Ryan

A love story of betrayal and redemption

Book Four in the Mated
Fortune Series

J.P. Mooney

DEDICATION

For the thrill seekers, daydreamers and romantics.

CONTENTS

Chapter One

Book Four

Ryan

I've been going crazy over the past few months. I don't know what I was thinking about leaving her at the train station like that when we both knew we were meant to be together. Maybe not forever like the typical love story, but at least for the foreseeable future. My reasoning behind my leaving was to keep her safe. There were people after me. Bad men who didn't care who they got their hands on as long as they got their money. And I owed them a lot of money. I knew Isabella was meant for me ever since the day I showed up bruised and bloody at Frank's apartment. It wasn't our finest hour. There was a dead body on his kitchen floor, Frank looked pale, and Izzy was trying to keep it together. This was the day she really stepped up for me. Sure, she had slept with my brother, killed him and then messed up my life by trying to kill me, too, but what is a relationship without a little bit of insanity to keep me alive? In truth, Andrew and I barely had a relationship. Especially when I discovered he was blackmailing women and spiralling out of control. Ever since we were little, I was constantly bailing him out of trouble, not just because I was his older brother but because ever since our mother abandoned us, I had a massive sense of responsibility for him. Sure, we were half-brothers, and neither of us knew our father. Nonetheless, we were brothers, and all we had was each other.

Many years later and Andrew still couldn't find his path in life. He had a great job, a steady girlfriend with her own ambitions. Somehow his void grew deeper, and he found solace in alcohol. Some days he would show up at my doorstep looking grey with his pupils dilated and cloudy. Like a hurricane waiting to destroy everything in its path. I would take him in and nurse him back to his grim reality. He would get up and swear he wouldn't take or drink anything again, but these promises were frequently broken until I got a frantic call from his girlfriend, Juliana. He had blacked out and trashed her apartment. She tried to leave, but he blackmailed her, so I told her to frame him for assault. It was the only way out for her, and although Andrew was my brother, I knew that the void inside him would only grow, and he would eventually get hurt or hurt someone.

I sensed that Juliana was an easy target. She was sweet, smart, and soft-spoken, with an incredible work ethic. Despite what Isabella thought was happening between her and me, Juliana became my friend. We were bonded for life because of Andrew. I was so pissed off at Frank and Izzy for drugging her. We all had our bad behaviours, but that was unacceptable. Still, it was interesting to see her get jealous. Even when our world was collapsing with packs of hyenas lurking in the shadows, a force pulled us towards each other. I was angry with her for trying to kill me. I would've been dead if I hadn't been smart enough to figure out what John and Andrew planned to do to her and what she had planned to get away with. My biggest mistake all those months ago was taking that drink from her. I knew she was up to something when I previously saw her, and luckily connections came in the room on time with a shot of adrenaline before her concoction knocked me out forever. I spared them the details; I just needed to get as far away from that hotel as possible.

From then, my life spiralled out of control. I couldn't go back to my job; I sunk deeper into the network of plugs for fake IDs and credit cards. I could've left the city and start a new life somewhere. I had always wanted to live in Devon, but my rage and thirst for revenge grew. I needed to make her suffer, so I got a room at Hotel Aldwych, where I had enough time to think and plan my revenge. I watched her socials and followed Frank around when I realised they were paranoid. They hadn't seen each other since the night John died, and they were waiting for it to blow over.

Fortunately for them, the hotel killed the story before it became one, courtesy of generous donations from The Wolf. They didn't want their brand associated with any negative press. John's employer also did the same, and I guess the company lurked in all sorts of secrets and malpractice. Everyone wanted to keep their hands clean. John's elderly parents were paid off, and since he had no siblings, they were happy with their luxurious retirement home. As for me, I was alone. Nobody knew about Andrew's death. Frank and Isabella made sure of that. Quite frankly, he was in a better place. I couldn't watch over him forever. At that point, as far as everyone was concerned, I disappeared. My stubbles grew, and my face was broken just like my heart. How could she do that to me? When I went to her room, I was trying to help her. I called Juliana and explained that I knew a woman who may have been another one of Andrew's victims and that she may need to seek refuge. I planned to get her somewhere outside the city, away from John. But it was too late. Isabella had already succumbed to her rage. I applauded her, though; she was a survivor.

In the den of lions and snakes, we all had to do what we needed to survive. It didn't take long for me to rattle her through messages and lure her to me. She thought she had the upper hand. And sure enough, we were back to our games. Then the real game players found me and beat the crap out of me for owing them money. This time Isabella came to my rescue, not once but twice. Throughout the cat and mouse chase, the push and pull of our relationship, I caught myself falling hard for her, although I didn't want to admit it to myself. And she didn't want to either. Eventually, I got the revenge I sought. It wasn't to kill her or turn her into the police. It was to break her heart. Despite everything we went through together, I needed to knock her off her horse. She got arrogant and thought she had me eating out of her palm just because she helped me, but deep down, I knew that whatever she did wasn't enough for me to let everything go. Frank had moved into his new apartment, and although I held indifference for him, it was hard to shake that no matter what I did for Isabella, he would always be her priority. We had talked about me leaving, and she kept her cool. It would happen regardless because I knew we couldn't be together without looking over our shoulders. The day she admitted her love for me, I knew that was my revenge. She had clung to the hope that I would change my mind. I'd grown to know her so well. She played it cool until that final moment at the train station when she professed her love for me. As strong as she thought she was, that was the moment

I saw her armour crack. She had hoped I would stay when she admitted her love for me. And still, I left.

That was then; months later, I felt ten pounds lighter. I don't know what she had been doing with her life other than I knew Frank made sure she was safe. We had agreed to keep in touch. He would drop me a message or a phone call here and there to let me know Isabella was alright. Eventually, those became less frequent. I assumed she had moved on. I, on the other hand, went through each day missing her. I didn't regret punishing her, but I also punished myself. Then, one Friday night, I got a call from Frank telling me that Izzy knew about our arrangement. He gave me an ultimatum: either I return home to her or leave her alone forever. The choice was simple. As much as I enjoyed the Devon air and the laid-back lifestyle, it was time for me to return to my girl. This time I was going back for good. Regardless of the challenges, I was willing to show her that I would be there for her.

I couldn't believe it. The apartment was still the same. Clean, tidy and full of life, just like her. She hadn't bothered to change the lock, but I was sure she would after finding out I kept a copy of her keys. There were muffled noises when I approached her door but then silence when I turned my keys in the lock. I stepped inside to find Frank and two unknown men standing in front of Isabella, ready for a fight. I didn't go there for a fight, but my heart ached when I saw how one of the men had his hand around her waist. I wanted to hurt him for touching her but then realised that she had moved on, although that didn't stop my longing for her. I wanted to leap by her side, hold her tight, and tell her that she was the missing part of my heart, but she stood frozen for a while. As though she had seen the ghost of Christmas past. Minutes later, we were in the kitchen as I explained why I was back. I couldn't help but shake the feeling that the new man in her life was eavesdropping our conversation. He had a look that didn't sit well with me, the business owner. Not a typical type for Izzy, considering her past choices, but it was typical for her to gravitate towards men with money. She thought she hid it well from me, but I knew what she did for a living. I had seen her on her dates long before our relationship evolved. As we stood in the kitchen, I heard Frank snap the men's attention back to drinking. At that moment, I knew that even if we weren't friends, there was a chance that he was betting on me.

Book Four

Chapter Two

Book Four

Isabella

My heart pounded, and with each breath, I felt my ribs constrict in apprehension. This couldn't be real. It felt like a dream. It must have been a dream. I closed my eyes and drew in a deep breath to try and centre my thoughts. When they opened, I knew this wasn't a dream. We had been standing in my living room for what felt like an eternity glaring at Ryan. Our eyes darted with questions. He looked different but the same. His muscles were larger and taut, his hair and skin glistened with vitality and his jaw, stubble-free chiselled to perfection. He looked more handsome than ever. Frank had leapt to my side while Mik and Nathan gave each other a confused look.

"Hi." Ryan cleared his throat.

"And you are?" Nathan asked without hesitation. The situation was beyond awkward.

"A close friend of Isabella's." He looked at me for confirmation, but I was still anchored in shock. I eventually snapped out of the trance.

"Why are you here? Are you in trouble?" My guard was up. He shook his head and walked to the kitchen. This was surreal. I excused myself and followed him while Frank did his best to compose Nathan and Mik. I heard him mutter something about Ryan being an old roommate, but I'm sure Mik remembered him from previous dealings.

"I came back because my life isn't right without you."
He whispered his response as though he knew I was
moving on with Nathan and didn't want to make a fuss.
I stepped back with my eyes searching for a glass to
pour myself a drink. I would've jumped into his arms a
few months ago and kissed him so hard that it hurt.
Now, I was angry that he decided to ruin the first
proper Christmas I had with Nathan and my friends.
Things were going great, and I didn't need further
complications. As I opened my mouth to respond,
Jules brushed himself against my ankle, meowing for
attention. "You got a cat?" A soft smile stretched
across his face.

"He's a rescue." I kept my answer short as I picked up
Jules and stroked his head. "I can't do this right now,
you better go." That was the truth, and he wasn't
pleased. I assumed he got himself a hotel, but for sure,
I wouldn't let him leave without giving back my house
keys.

"Fine, here's my new number. Please call me soon so
we can talk. I'm not giving up on you, Izzy." My heart
sank because I would've given anything to hear those
words a few months ago. A lot has happened since
then. Frank and I had to focus on our new findings
without further distractions. I took the paper from his
hand and walked him to the door.

"My keys." He reluctantly handed them to me, but my
face was stern. Then he left.

I approached the living room to find Frank doing shots
with Nathan and Mik. He attempted to distract them

while I dealt with Ryan. By that point, though, I decided to join them. It wasn't the right time to talk or address the situation, and I made sure that Nathan understood that when he began to prompt with questions. I would explain my relationship with Ryan to him eventually, but for now, drinking myself into amnesia was the motive for the rest of the night. Soon enough, the memory of Mik dancing around the apartment with Jules in his arms was embedded in my mind, and my numbness settled on my lips. It was the warmest Christmas I had ever experienced in my entire adulthood.

Nathan decided to cook breakfast the following day since we were all hungover. I couldn't stomach the smell of a full fry-up, so I opted for a green smoothie and some toast while everyone else salivated at the greasy plates of food served. There was no mention of Ryan's rather rude interruption to our night, and since my head was fragile, I was okay with that. Frank decided to hack his system with an upper that made its way back up his stomach. This kind of hangover wasn't to be hacked; we all had no choice but to ride through it. The rest of the day was spent in relaxation. Nathan had brought a change of clothes, while Frank had to share his emergency sleepover outfits with Mik. Mik didn't look too awkward in them since they were about the same size. But their taste in fashion was definitely different. Frank was more put together, while Mik had more edge, although they complimented each other. While Frank and Mik chatted and sipped their beverages, Nathan and I decided to retreat to the comfort of my bedroom. That was when he decided to bring up the dreaded subject of Ryan.

"That man was more than a friend, right?" I stayed silent for a moment as I carefully crafted my response. "Come on, Izzy. I'm not stupid; I saw your reaction." I wasn't ready to deal with this, but I guess it was better to discuss it now rather than later.

"He broke my heart." Of all the answers I could've given, I chose to leap with vulnerability. "We had a whirlwind romance, and it ended with him leaving. I swear I don't even remember giving him a copy of my keys. I never thought I'd see him again, and he confessed his love for me last night." There it was, my honesty exposed for him to play with.

"And do you love him?" Was he serious? He said himself that he saw my reaction the night before; of course, I still loved Ryan.

"Of course, I do. He was my first true love." Nathan pinched the bridge of his nose and closed his eyes. I thought he was going to break, but he held himself well. However, I couldn't be blamed for my answer since he asked the question and expected nothing but honesty. "But the most important thing right now is that I'm with you, and that's not changing." I thought this statement would soften the blow of my revelation, but then Nathan stood up and walked to my en suite bathroom. No doubt he would leave, but I wouldn't stop him. Sometimes people just needed space to process their thoughts, and I was beginning to understand that. So I sat on my bed and waited for him to announce his exit. I waited ten minutes before he emerged from the bathroom with his arms crossed across his chest as though he had been summoned to a meeting.

"I told you I wanted to be in your life no matter what. Friends with benefits or otherwise, we have grown closer over the last few days. But I can't be here waiting for you to toss me aside when you decide to be with Ryan." I moved towards him, and for once, I felt myself soften, like really soften. My heart opened, and I knew that despite my past, Nathan was who I was meant to spend my time with in the present. He was kind, patient and uncomplicated. I felt at ease around him, and that was important. He was right, we had grown closer over the past few days, and it didn't alarm me.

"Nathan, you're being melodramatic." I grinned. "We are evolving into something good here, and I don't want to lose that, okay. I don't want Ryan. I want what we have right now. So, chill. Let's just enjoy the process." With that, he smiled and reclined on the bed next to me. My life was far from perfect, but I was in heaven when I got to snuggle in his arms and soak up his warmth.

The following days were busy. Frank returned to his usual shifts at the gallery, and I went on a few dates with three clients. The time between Christmas and New Year was great for work since my clients were back in their offices, trying to muster excitement and motivation to end the year on a high and enter the new year with higher expectations. This expected they had to schedule last-minute business dinners to secure all the important contracts. Which meant they would book me as a visual appeal to encourage their potential partners. I thought about increasing my prices around this time but soon realised there was no need since my clients were exceptionally generous with their tips and always paid for all expenses associated with the date. At the end of each date, I would have large sums of money to wire into my offshore accounts. You may wonder whether I had enough to quit doing what I do, and the answer is yes. However, I enjoyed having the power that came with my job. I loved the notion of building wealth for myself and having the freedom to do whatever I wanted. Money wasn't an issue on a day-to-day, but I knew too well that my criminal lifestyle would catch up with me, and there'll be a day when I would have to disappear, leaving everything behind to start a new life. I was playing chess with life. That transition had to be smooth and comfortable for me, and that would require a large amount of wealth.

Nathan returned to his townhouse and attended to his business as usual. His customers were happy, and the restaurant was thriving. Our friends-with-benefit situation was going smoothly, and so far, no pressure or feelings forced us into uncharted territory. Life was easy, but my guard was still up, and so was Frank's. Since Nathan and Mik had returned to living their lives, we had started digging through the documents and pictures from Detective Johnson's house. Nothing was mentioned in the news about her death, but Frank and I knew that people were out there watching us. It was only a matter of time before they came knocking at the door. But I had planned to find them first. Each night

I worked meticulously to study the documents and photographs and, so far, had found nothing of significance. Although, I didn't fret because I had time, and things had always worked out in my favour so far.

Book Four

Chapter Three

Book Four

Isabella

I opted for a form-fitting beige dress with nude heels while my eyes fluttered with fake eyelashes and smoky eyeshadow. Frank had booked tickets for a musical and insisted we go with Mik and Nathan. I rolled my eyes at his suggestion since we had spent Christmas together and thought celebrating New Year's Eve with my best friend was a solid mark for the next chapter of our lives. However, I couldn't argue with him since it was positive that we both had people in our lives that grounded us with normality. Besides, our friendship was strong, and I didn't want us to revert to our old co-dependent ways.

"So, how's counselling going with Doctor Chris?" I asked as I fastened a necklace around my neck. Frank didn't want to return to Doctor Chris after what we discovered at Detective Johnson's house, but he continued his appointments with my encouragement.

"Really good but I didn't know that I had so many underlying issues." His smirk reflected in the mirror of my vanity.

"Don't we all." I returned his smile. "How's things with you and Mik?" This was a touchy subject. Although they weren't private about showing each other affection, Frank barely spoke about the intimate details of his relationship with Mik. I suspected it was because they never had the 'what is this' conversation, and he didn't want whatever it was they were doing to be defined.

"It's good. He's nothing like I thought he was."

"I think a lot of people would say the same thing about you. On the outside you look big and distant." I teased. "But, on the inside you are such a mushy teddy." He shook his head and rolled his eyes.

"Well, it's a good thing not many people know me. Izzy, it's nearly 6 p.m. Hurry up so we can leave. I don't want us to be late. The queue to the bar gets busy in theatres. Fifteen minutes later, we both descended to the street and got into a cab smelling like the expensive outcasts we were.

As much as I hated to admit it, Frank was right. The queues to the ticket office, bar and ladies were busy. Although to our delight, Nathan had already picked up the tickets and bought a decanter of Chardonnay. Mik greeted us with a big smile as he held onto the snacks he'd stuffed in a small bag. All the men in my presence looked handsome in formal shirts and tailored trousers. I felt safe and proud. Nathan and I had discussed our New Year's Eve plans and pondered whether we were making the right decision to spend it together, but I chose to be honest with myself. Yes, we were in a friend-with-benefit situation, yet we grew closer each day. The only thing that stood in the way of us being together were my secrets. I learned not to get too comfortable with Nathan, like the men before him; I couldn't entirely give him my trust. For now, though, I decided to relax and enjoy what I had before it disappeared. Because eventually, Frank and I knew that the new year would bring a new depth of chaos.

"Are you okay?" Nathan pulled me back into focus.

"Yeah, it's just hot in here." We went ahead to our seats.

The show was great; the actors kicked and danced across the stage with precision, although I was glad to have picked the seat next to Frank while Nathan sat on my right side. I got mildly bored after a while and was thankful for the intermission to check my phone and replenish my wine. Remembering how busy the ladies were, I quickly grabbed my bag and went to the bathroom. We planned to all meet back at our seats. I managed to be the first to use the ladies, although the first thing I did was grab my phone to check my emails and text messages. When I finished, I freshened up, touched up my lipstick and returned to my seat. Just as I opened the door to the foyer, a man caught my attention, or rather, I seemed to have caught his attention. His eyes looked familiar, and my instinct told me he was trouble. When he was about to say something, Frank appeared from the shadow and grabbed my hand. The man scurried away.

"Who the hell was that?" I whispered to Frank.

"I don't know, but I came over as quickly as I saw you two. Ghosts are lurking everywhere." We were back in our seats, waiting for the show's second part to begin, although, by that point, I just wanted to leave. Something about that man wasn't right, and I didn't want Nathan in a situation that would compromise his safety. As the rest of the show went on, Frank and I exchanged regular glares while we sat with tensed shoulders. We scanned the theatre to catch another look at the strange man and occasionally sipped our wine. Nathan and Mik looked excited as they slyly swayed to the music. And by the time Frank and I finished the last drop of Chardonnay from the decanter, the actors were at their curtain call. Thank goodness! At this point, Frank and I were successfully merry, and we needed some food.

The mysterious man was nowhere to be seen after the show, so Frank and I shrugged him off as we went to an Italian restaurant for food. The night was still young, but after seeing that man, I was reminded that my apartment was the only place I felt safe. Frank had the same idea as he yawned while waiting for the food to arrive. As fun, as it was to hang out with Mik and Nathan, we both knew that we weren't the type of people who celebrated New Year's Eve like the rest of the world. We were content with sharing a joint, ordering in and drinking bourbon until we passed out because we both knew that each year would bring a new form of chaos. Nathan and Mik had been sweet, bonding over their experience with Jules. Every time Mik came over, he had brought a bag of toys and treats while Nathan got ample snuggles in before he left for work in the mornings. I was beginning to convince myself that he only stuck around because he liked the kitten more than me. I smiled to myself at that thought. We made small talk over dinner, and although my body was at the table, my mind was far out, wondering about him. Ryan. So many times, I had thought to message him, but I couldn't trust myself to be around him. Just because he decided to come back and claim me, it didn't mean that I had to change my life to be with him.

I liked Nathan, and I couldn't throw what we had away for someone who chose to leave me after I confessed my love for him.

Nonetheless, I longed for him. I wanted to know where he was staying and hoped it wasn't the same hotel; he chose to seek refuge after my failed attempt to kill him. My legs shook under the table as I began to wonder about him. I was agitated by his distraction, and Nathan knew it when he lightly placed his hand on my knee. I pulled myself back into the room when I realised Frank and Mik were missing.

"They went to the bar for shots." Nathan confirmed as though he had read my mind.

"Oh, right."

"Is this too much?" Of course it was too much. I wasn't a traditional woman. I grew up collecting bricks around my heart to protect myself. My sanity and tolerance for this world hung by a thread. I lived every day like it was my last because it could be. I slept with wealthy men for a living while I calculated every aspect of my exit plan for when I would eventually need to cut ties with this city. Yet, here I was, having dinner two hours before entering the new year with a man I couldn't bring myself to completely let into my heart because it belonged to someone else. Too much was a drop in a bucket compared to the totality of my messed-up life.

"It's just, I don't usually do this with men unless they're paying me well. I don't like the traditional new year's celebrations. It feels too much like we're a couple." My words were sharp, but the last thing I wanted was to hurt Nathan's feelings. Although at that point, my mind was made up.

"Hey, I understand." He was too sweet. "I thought it would be too much for us, and it's okay if you want to go home. I'm actually tired. That show was longer than it needed to be." Surprised, I leaned in and kissed his lips. Something I rarely did in public. Minutes later, I bid my farewell to Mik and Frank, whose eyes were now lazy and speech slurred. I chuckled at Frank's choice of beverage, a woo-woo with a green umbrella. I knew he would regret drinking that in the morning since sugary cocktails with syrupy E-numbers were the devil to him. For now, though, I let him have his fun. He deserved it.

"Look after him Mik." I whispered in his ear and kissed his cheek. *What an interesting turn of events.* I smiled at the thought.

Nathan had ordered a taxi and offered to pay, while he made me promise to text him as soon as I got home. "I'm heading home too, so I'll see you drunken sailors soon." He aimed at Frank and Mik, then walked me to the taxi bay outside the restaurant. I arrived home just after 11 p.m. and kicked my heels off at the door. I messaged Nathan to tell him I was home safe with a selfie. It was unnecessary, but I decided to be nice in the spirit of New Year's Eve. I stripped out of my dress and went to the bathroom, where I took off my makeup and got in the shower. I lathered and rinsed my night away, then patted myself dry and moisturised my face and body. I enveloped my body in a fresh bathrobe, then rummaged in the kitchen for a glass of wine. I looked at the clock; it was three minutes to midnight. Fireworks were displayed all over the city. This wasn't my first new year without Frank, but I really missed him. It was so good to see him happy, and I hoped he stayed with Mik for a while.

Ryan

I honestly wasn't expecting to hear from her since Christmas day, but the moment I got her message, I was on my feet, ready to be with her.

Come over.

It could've been a setup, but I didn't care. If Isabella was ready to talk, I would happily drop whatever I was doing for her. Not that I had grand plans anyway. Years ago, I would spend New Year's Eve getting tipsy in bars looking for any woman to take home with me for the night just to feel wanted. Since the Lake District incident, I was happy to stay inside and sleep early. Which was what I had planned before receiving her message. When I arrived on Christmas day, I booked the closest Bed & Breakfast in Shoreditch I could find at the last minute.

The room was modest, but for the last-minute rate, I couldn't complain. I was at her door just five minutes after midnight. Adrenaline coursed in my veins that I couldn't remember how I got there, whether I flew, jogged or took a taxi. I lightly tapped her door, and she opened it with a straight face. We smiled awkwardly at each other, and within seconds, she was loosening the belt on her robe. I certainly wasn't there for that, but seeing her body in its glorious perfection reminded me of what I was missing. And she knew this too. Her cruel punishment, she loved to tease me. She turned and walked to the kitchen while I followed behind, ensuring the door was locked. She poured a glass of wine and held out the glass; I hesitated. She put her lips to the glass and drained the ruby-red liquid. She poured some more, and this time, I accepted the glass and took a big gulp of the wine.

Whatever was happening was going to be slow and painful for me. We stood there slowly sipping our wine, exchanging lustful glances at each other. The veins on my arms and neck raised with anticipation; my manhood was already rock hard just seeing the curves of her breasts peek through the open slit of her robe. I wanted her just like the first time I saw her. Back then, she had a playful innocence about her, and now, she was about to make me pay for leaving her. And I wanted to pay her with my hands, my fingers and my mouth on her skin, neck and thighs. My skin prickled with heat as the wine swirled to my head. I placed the glass down and slowly walked towards her. She opened herself and leaned back on the counter, inviting me into her bubble of devilish softness. My face tilted towards her lips as I towered over her, and she looked up, searching my eyes. I don't know what she was looking for, but I saw her vulnerability for a moment, so I took her bottom lip into my mouth. We were instantly fused together in our fiery pit of lust. Our kiss grew deeper and hungrier, biting to the point of drawing blood, primal like lions' mating ritual. Her back was still arched on the kitchen counter as I traced my lips down her body until I reached the soft spot between her thighs. My hands firmly held her thigh on my shoulder as my mouth parted to let my tongue give her the pleasure she deserved. Her soft moans grew louder as she sunk her fingers in and grabbed my hair every time my tongue grazed her bud. We were exactly how we'd been but better. This time, we were both hungrier and dared to push the limits. The louder her moan got, the more my tongue swirled around her until I did what she liked, to push her closer to the edge. I lightly took her between my teeth, and her body jolted with pleasure while her hand grabbed harder at my hair.

"Don't stop." She breathed.

I wasn't stopping and wouldn't leave her apartment until she got the pleasure she demanded. I continued to work my mouth on her until her breath quickened and her skin grew hot with lust. She pulled me up to her level and once again kissed me with need while my hands caressed her body. She shrugged off her robe and opened herself to invite me in, taking me in her hand to rub against her wetness. She knew how to tease and torment me, and I let her do so until I couldn't take it anymore. I grabbed a condom from my wallet and slowly slid inside her while a moan escaped her mouth. A few hours ago, I was ready to enter the new year alone in my bed, and now I was making love to Isabella on her kitchen counter. My mind collapsed as we got lost in the darkness of our pleasure. Lips leeched onto one another as I held her tight while I made love to her, slow and deep. Her arousal brought me to new heights, and I never wanted to let her go. But I couldn't hold on any longer, and fortunately, we both got our release with exquisite timing. My heart began to slow, and my thoughts, although cloudy, oriented back to us. My hands found their way up to her face, that glistened with sweat. We were stuck in a blissful moment, and neither of us wanted to let go. She may have been with that other guy, but I knew she wanted me. I could feel it on her chest, where I placed a hand to feel her heartbeat. Moments later, we sat on her sofa, drinking the rest of the wine. Seeped in silence that was occasionally broken by the sparks of fireworks outside. It was just after 1 a.m., and I sensed her regret, but I would be damned if I chose to leave her again. Isabella would have to throw me out with force.

"Well, that was something." She finally spoke.

"You are something Isabella." I leaned in and kissed her forehead. A gesture that successfully made her flush.

"This didn't mean anything. I was horny and you were available." That was a lie, and we both knew it, but I gave her a pass.

"What about your boyfriend?" I shamelessly batted the question, and she raised an eyebrow debating her answer.

"He's not my boyfriend. Anyway, it's none of your business."

"I'm making it my business." She rolled her eyes in irritation. I hated when we bickered like this. It was such a waste of time. I dropped the subject. We sipped the rest of our wine in silence when she finally stretched out a yawn and invited me into her bed. My heart raced as I followed her to the bedroom and climbed under the warm duvet. I just got my life back, but I knew it would quickly descend into chaos as her gravity pulled me into her licentious quicksand. There was more than one man. The ones who paid her well were Nathan, the sweet gentleman, Frank, the best friend, and then there was me. The one who matched the broken shards of her heart.

Chapter Four

Book Four

Isabella

Was it wise to invite Ryan in for a night of passion? No. Did I have fun and woke up satisfied? Absolutely. The thought of entering the new year alone made me feel empty, and I was tired of finding mindful ways to fill my void. I needed a sound wave to surf, and Ryan was just the wave I sought. His hands, lips and mouth felt how I remembered, and I would lie if I thought it wouldn't happen again. This situation was simple. I could disconnect myself from Nathan and focus on mending a relationship with Ryan since I've longed for him for months. However, I wasn't ready to give in to him just yet. I couldn't let him think that he could run away and snap my heart back to him like he owned it. I had to make him work for it, and I needed to know that he wouldn't leave me again because, this time, I didn't think I could get through it. Having him in my bed poured a comfort I yearned for, and I wanted him to stay. I rolled off the bed to find his side empty. My heart raced, expecting his impromptu departure. I quickly draped my naked body in my silk robe and went to the kitchen to find him making pancakes.

"You need to go grocery shopping. Your fridge is empty." He smiled and continued to cook the batter as I stood close by. I didn't know what to say then, but I was conscious of my ease around him.

We ate pancakes on my balcony and watched the Shoreditch inhabitants enter their new year's resolutions. The palpable silence between us grew thicker with each passing minute until I couldn't take it anymore. It was time for him to leave.

"So you're telling me that you got out of last night's festivities early so that you could sleep with Ryan?" Frank scowled across his dining table as he held onto his cup of coffee. He winced when I giggled.

"I didn't ditch you Frank. You and Mik disappeared to the bar first so technically, you left me. Anyway, that's not the point. I just felt so off being there with Nathan, so tamed and reserved."

"Do you want to be with Ryan?" The question should've caught me off guard, but it didn't. I wanted to be with Ryan, but I was hesitant. Frank waited patiently for a response that never came, but he knew me well enough to guess my thoughts. "Well this coffee isn't doing anything for my head. Let's go out for lunch, I can do with a fatty fry-up and a smoothie. My treat."

We left his apartment, walked to our local café and parked ourselves in a small booth. Frank ordered food but glared at me while we waited for it to arrive. "What now?" I asked, half smirking.

"You still haven't answered my question and we should at least explore what's happening here." He shrugged.

"Of course I want to be with him. But did you forget how deep we are in this mess? I don't need to be dragged to a toxic situation for him to leave again." The food arrived just as I was about to open my mouth once more. The conversation quickly fell into silence as Frank shoved the fry-up in his mouth. I sipped my smoothie and took a bite of pastry.

"No, I haven't forgotten. I just don't think he'll leave you again, Izzy. He's madly in love with you!" He said with a theatrical voice. "Anyway, he's here now, and you slept with him. We both know it'll happen again. He smirked.

We spent the rest of the morning chatting about life until we decided to return to our apartments so that Frank could sleep off the rest of his hangover. On the other hand, I thought it was a good time to change and go for a long run, as I believed it would be good to start the year right. When I returned home, my heart felt like it would collapse onto itself, and I began to regret pushing myself too hard on the run. The clock in the bathroom read 2 p.m. so I decided to take my time scrubbing my skin in the shower, but really, it was a futile prolonged distraction to get Ryan out of my mind. Every time I directed my mind to think about solving the mysteries of blackmailing and The Wolf, Ryan managed to creep into the crevices of my memories. When I got dressed, my stomach started grumbling, so I ordered some sushi and wrapped up the administration for my clients. I had guaranteed clients booked for the first half of the year, and despite them being the usual, I still had to vet each one for safety. Once I finished, the food arrived, and it was time to remedy my hunger.

I looked at the documents from Detective Johnson's house as I chomped down on my lunch. This was the fiftieth time that I studied them; most times, it was with

Frank's help. But now, as I stared at the photographs, handwritten notes and receipts, I sunk deeper into wondering what the point was to all of it.

Rage. That's all I felt as I scrolled through the pictures. I should be devoid of any feelings in this situation, but as I scrolled through the pictures on her social media account, I felt jealousy creep in and cloud my judgment. The entire time I thought about how stupid I had been, believing that he came back to be with me and now, as I saw him smiling with his arms around the woman, my heart frosted over as my trust for Ryan ran cold. I rationalised that he had left months ago and would meet someone uncomplicated to be with, even if it was just for a while. But knowing what I knew about him and as the memories of past circumstances that plagued us floated in my mind, I knew that nothing was ever innocent with Ryan. Even back when we first met, everything was premeditated. I didn't know who this woman was. Her profile flagged up as someone I may have known, and it was public, so I thought I'd have a snoop. Ryan didn't seem to mind her posting the picture online; he liked it. A risky move in our world, but I guess she was worth taking the risk for.

I had spent the rest of the afternoon in a daze, infused with silent rage. Frank was still sleeping off his hangover, so I refrained from waking him up, especially while I was not operating from a sound mind. In my true style, I decided to smoke a joint and pour myself a tipple of bourbon. Instantly my vision elevated, and my heart rate slowed enough for my body to relax. I sat on the kitchen island, and a picture from the Detective's documents immediately caught my attention. I hadn't noticed any of the people in there, but as I looked closer at the brunette whose green eyes reflected back at me, I knew she was the same woman from the picture with Ryan. My heart rate picked up just in time with my rage, and I cursed myself for letting my guard down. I didn't know what role this woman had to play in this blackmailing ring, nor did I understand her connection to 'The Wolf', but either way, I found myself a lead.

"Izzy, this better be good. Give me ten minutes." Frank's response was quick. Soon enough, we were settled on the kitchen island, nursing some bourbon. "I can't believe it. This is not an innocent connection, but we need to find out how deep it goes. I'll ask Mik to do some digging. But you must consider the possibility that he's playing you, he might even be in love with this woman."

"Or maybe she's using him?" Hope entangled my words as I shook the image of him with her out of my mind. The positive about this was now we had someone to look into that could lead us closer to the linchpin that held this game together.

By the time darkness fell over the city, we had found where the woman in the photo was based. She was registered as a stakeholder in an office in Oxford Circus. "Something to do with fashion." Mik had confirmed when he told Frank the address. We decided to get as much information on her as possible, and we were ready to pay her a visit early the next day. Frank decided to crash at my apartment, and I welcomed the company as I couldn't trust myself to not call Ryan. The following day, we were both on our feet, dressed in our finest outfits in the taxi to Oxford Circus. The ride was quiet as I coached myself to keep it together. It was then that I realised that I wasn't afraid of the outcome; I was afraid of losing control and ruining everything for me and Frank.

The building of her registered office was under the name Clara Wayde although I doubted she would register her real name on public domains. People like us were too calculated for such errors. Mik also booked me an appointment as a potential investor. I don't know how he pulled such a string to make it believable, and I would never ask since this was his profession. I just trusted his information was correct, and I remembered my cues. Frank wanted to come in with me, but I wanted to get a look at Clara alone without distraction.

"Text me if you need me. I mean it Izzy, don't get ahead of yourself."

"I won't." I smiled and entered the building.

The reception was standard, furnished with black leather chairs and glass desks. Distracted with boredom, the receptionist assigned my visitor's badge and instructed me to take the lift to the second floor. I exited the lift to meet another receptionist, only this time, she looked like she enjoyed her job. The office was decorated with a feminine touch accentuated by the sunlight that beamed through the big windows. Just as I was about to sit on the plush-looking sofa, her familiar face emerged from the corridor. Her malachite-coloured dress gave her a polished look as her dark hair clung to her shoulder. She was even more attractive in person. "Jane Johnson?" I gave her an authentic smile as she approached and beckoned me for a handshake. She didn't let on that she knew of me, nor did I of her. We made our way to her office, which presented a stunning view of the city, but I was quickly distracted by questions that surfed my mind. Her connection with Ryan was possibly innocent, but I knew better than to sit in trust.

"So, tell me about your proposal?" She quickly snapped me out of my thoughts. I rattled on about my fake proposal just like I rehearsed with Frank; all the while, Clara sat and listened intently. I watched her face for signs that she knew about me beforehand, but her poker face demeanour didn't falter. Before I knew it, thirty minutes had passed, and the meeting was over. She thanked me again for my time, and I discreetly made my way out of the office, seizing the opportunity to grab one of her business cards from her desk. Outside, the street is littered with people from all walks of life. Men in business suits, tourists and shoppers floated by as my heart raced and my shoulders hung heavier than at the start of the day.

"So?" Frank waited patiently as I caught my breath.

"Nothing. She didn't let anything slip Frank. But I did take this." Showing him the business card. "Maybe we can find out more based on this information."

"I'll see if the guys can bring up records of her phone calls." He said coolly.

"They can do that?" Surprised and suddenly felt like an amateur when it came to using technology.

"Of course they can babe. They can do anything, although you know by now that it won't be cheap. We'll get closer to what we're looking for Izzy. Let's get some lunch. I could also use a drink."

We parked ourselves in a quaint restaurant not too far from Clara's office. This was somewhat strategic, as I hoped she would walk by at some point looking for somewhere to grab lunch. Frank talked, but I didn't listen. My eyes stayed glued on the busy street. Frank eventually stopped talking, and we grew silent with the low chatter of the restaurant surrounding us. Back in my apartment, I searched the internet for anything related to the information on Clara's business card to no avail. The picture of her and Ryan illuminated on my phone screen, so I poured myself a glass of wine and sipped quickly until my head stirred. Eventually, the bottle stood empty on the coffee table, just like the hole that grew in my chest.

Chapter Five

Book Four

Isabella

At sixteen, ever since my life turned upside down, I isolated myself from others. Perhaps it was unconscious, but I stopped checking on friends and relatives because I felt nobody cared about me. This was a precedence to the way I isolated myself in adulthood. People always wanted to harvest something from me. My energy, my company or my intelligence. I grew up before my time, and it wasn't always easy. My first night alone in London was one of the scariest yet most empowering feelings I experienced. And now, in the moment of confusion, I welcomed that feeling. For the first time in a while, I felt powerless, and I didn't know if it was the fact that I gave my heart to a man who could potentially be involved in my demise or that I was slowly throwing away a man who really accepted me with my limitations. As my mind swirled in a dark fog, I sent a message and waited for a response.

Need to see you.

An hour later, he sat on my bed with his hand running through my hair as a tear ran down my cheek. Nathan was always there when I needed him, and I felt guilty for the way I left him on New Year's Eve. I didn't tell him I slept with Ryan, not because I felt guilty as we weren't in a relationship but because I wasn't prepared to deal with follow-up questions about where that left us. And deep down, I was afraid of losing what we had, whatever it was.

"I think you may have drunk a little too much." I stared at him, although my lids were slightly swollen. "You don't have to talk right now. I'm here for as long as you need me." He gave me a smile that instantly uplifted my soul. I wanted to find a way to tell him everything, unload my darkest secrets, and, for once, feel the weight lift off my shoulders. Regardless of what I wanted, the secrets I kept weren't just mine; they were Frank's. Besides, Nathan was nice, but we lived in different worlds, and someone like him would probably go straight to the police. That's how I rationalised my lack of trust.

That night, Nathan and I slept in the same bed without sleeping together. Our bodies were entangled in a warmth that gave me temporary comfort and security. And long after he slipped into a deep sleep, I lay awake trying to put pieces of my life together and understand why certain situations unravelled the way they did until I eventually succumbed to sleep.

It was 3 a.m. when I got a call from Frank to meet him outside my apartment building since Nathan was still in my bed, and I didn't want him to hear our conversation. His voice sounded urgent. I quickly dressed and went downstairs, where he stood with Mik looking glum.

"Have you spoken to Ryan about the picture?" He was straight to the point.

"No, not yet. I didn't know how to bring it up."

"Isabella, we managed to track Clara's phone records. Don't ask us how, it's too long to explain." Mik spoke. "Most of her calls were to Ryan and someone else in the past seventy-two hours. The picture, the calls and now that he's suddenly back in your life. It's not a coincidence. You need to speak to him." He continued. "I'm not saying he's part of this, but he's connected to someone who's connected to The Wolf. In my world, he's guilty by association regardless." My head spun. I knew this was coming, but this wasn't Frank talking. These words came from Mik, and he was damn good at his job.

"Okay, so maybe they're just fucking?" I asked, trying to suppress my denial. "You said there was another number. Who's was it?"

He took out a piece of paper and showed it to me. A man, well dressed in a blue suit, holding a briefcase in one hand and a phone in the other. I studied the image, but he didn't look familiar.

"This man was seen at detective Johnson's house the week before we went there. My guys hacked into her home CCTV, and he's been there quite frequently. He has people in his circle involved in drug trafficking, blackmail, arms dealing and money laundering. We've tracked his moves since you found the picture of Clara. She's met with him a few times and once right after you went to her office. That's not a coincidence either. We believe this is The Wolf."

"So, Ryan's involved in all this then."

"Not only that but these people were also connected to the detective. There might be others working on the inside to cover his tracks. Ryan could also be working with them or playing both sides, he's been in trouble before, and he even admitted that he had friends who helped him out of that hotel in the Lake District. That's my theory, but whatever the truth is, you need to be careful." Frank put his arm around me as we stood in silence. It's as if, deep down, I knew this would come. I knew I resisted Ryan's return for good reason; something didn't sit right in my intuition. Sure, there were a million explanations for this revelation, and I was probably a small portion of The Wolf's list of nuisances. Still, I potentially killed some of his people, tried to kill Ryan, and made a bit of a mess in his city. Regardless of whatever was happening, Ryan was connected to these people, and I was alert. Moments later, I thanked Mik for everything he'd done, told Frank I'd come by his apartment in the morning and made my way back to bed. Nathan, oblivious to what's happened, stirred in his sleep. I held him tight as though it was our last night together. He didn't deserve to be dragged into this, and I vowed that whatever happened from then on, I'd make sure he was safe. Our connection was the only logical and normal thing I had in my life. I couldn't destroy that.

"Nathan, we need to talk." I didn't mean for the words to come out so dramatic nonetheless, it had to be done. I told him that we couldn't see each other anymore and that it would be best to pretend that whatever we had never happened.

"Why are you doing this? What's changed?" His eyes glistened as he spat the questions to my ears. I knew he wouldn't give up on me easily, so I used the harshest weapon I had. My words.

"I don't need a reason to do this. Don't you get it? I don't want you. I was bored, you knew I would slip away eventually so save us both the energy. I don't want to see you anymore." Shock, rage and hurt plastered his face while I buried my regret deep in the hole of my chest.

"You're a real piece of work Isabella. You have no fucking clue how bad you've hurt me." He grabbed his things and went towards the door, slamming it on his exit. I had no choice but to get him as far away from me as possible. We'd meet again at a different time, in another life. For now, I pushed the feeling of loss deep and poured my tears into a glass of bourbon. Even if it was only 9 a.m.

By lunchtime, I was lost in my thoughts as I reclined on Frank's bed. I knew what I needed to do, but hesitation grew on me. Frank did everything to rationalise Ryan's involvement with Clara, but regardless of the reason, he was, in fact, still involved. Like Mik said, guilty by association. Minutes flew at a turtle pace as my chest grew and collapsed with disappointment. I felt stupid for believing he came to be with me, and I even thought we might have a future. It served me right for having my cake and wanting to eat it too.

"You and Mathew, me and Nathan, Andrew, Mathew and Darien." Frank glared at me with confusion. "What was the point of it all?" We fell into a silence that grew thick as we pondered our lives.

"Look, I didn't want to bring this up in front of Mik." He sat beside me, so close I could feel the hairs and warmth from his arm. "We've spent the past year getting ourselves together, stashing money, new identities and our escape route. You don't have to deal with any of this."

"What, and that's it? We just leave everything we've worked hard to build behind. Is this the breaking point?"

"I don't know. Look at you." I turned to the window and soaked in the city's landscape, embellished by the afternoon sun. A rare sight in late winter. He placed a thumb under my chin and gently turned my face to him. "This is the lowest I've ever seen you. I'm afraid you may not have enough gut to proceed with this, Izzy. Say the word, and we leave. Me and you." I was touched by his commitment to me. Frank was my family. I would die for him, but I couldn't take him away from the good thing he's found with Mik.

"I know you would. But this is not the breaking point because once we leave, we leave for good. I'm not ready to give up on our lives. I'm finishing this." We sat in embrace looking as ridiculous as we've always been together, only this time we were at matching heights. I don't know what our lives were unravelling into, but whatever it was, I would end it.

I arranged to have dinner with Ryan at his bed and breakfast. Frank thought it was a terrible idea that Ryan would catch on to what I was doing, but I thought it was good to be in his space so that he was comfortable. The room was leaning on dingey than chic, which was definitely a downgrade from his suite at Hotel Aldwych. Although back then, that was another life. I opted for a modest pencil skirt and satin blouse paired with nude heels. My red lipstick commanded the attention of everyone as soon as I left my apartment. I sipped my wine as I sat on the small armchair in the corner that provided a street view from the small window. Ryan sat on the bed and observed me. His hair, freshly trimmed, showcasing his beautiful face that was now stubble free.

"You're prompt, as usual." He smiled. "And may I say perhaps slightly overdressed for this environment. He teased, but I knew he liked what I was wearing.

We sat in silence as the tension between us grew. Partly from lust and my knowing that this was the last time I'd see him like this. Frank advised against seeing him, but given that I was going to light our lives on fire, I needed to be with him one last time to remember us in this state of innocence.

Ryan

Something was off with her, I knew it, but I couldn't point out what it was. This wasn't anything new. Isabella and I had been playing this chasing game since the day we met. So I sat on the bed and let her lead. I figured she would tell me eventually. Seeing her sitting in my room brought light to my life, and I couldn't process how much I missed her. Before I knew it, she was sitting on the edge of my bed with her hand cupping my cheek. And in a short time, I was undressing her. The world stopped momentarily as we explored each other's chaos with our tongues. I've held her many times before, but this time it felt like the realest and closest we've ever connected. My hand glided and studied every curve of her body. Every crevice was perfectly carved, and still, the physical representation of her beauty wasn't displayed with justice. Isabella was ethereal. She was addictive, and I was hooked. My mouth couldn't get enough of tasting her skin, her lips and between her thighs. And because I knew this couldn't last, that it was too good to be true, I took a mental picture of us here on my shitty bed to be framed in my memories forever. This picture would get me through the darkest of days.

"I love the warmth of your skin." She spoke while her head rested on my chest. I wanted to tell her I was warm because she revived my heart to exude warmth. Instead, I chose to respond with silence, cautious not to ruin the moment with silly words while I breathed in the rose scent from her luscious curls.

Hours passed. Even though I knew she wasn't sleeping over, I held her tighter in silent protest every time she stirred. As we rested there, I allowed my mind to roam into the uncharted territory of us even when I knew that with our lifestyle, there could never really be a way for us to be together without looking over our shoulders. And then there was the Nathan guy, whom I'm sure would probably be a better fit to keep her stable. Isabella has lived her entire adult life-fighting. She needed someone to ground her. On the other hand, I got myself into some deep complications that I couldn't let her get involved in. But in this moment of bliss and peace, I thought about what life would be like being with her boyfriend, husband and even the father of her child. Who was I fooling? I grunted. We're not kids' people. The kitten was cute, though, so that would suffice. We could add a puppy to the picture. A silly grin stretched on my face.

"What are you grinning about?"

"Nothing. Just thinking how great this is."

She lifted her head, and our eyes connected. I wanted to lead with my insanity. To propose to her right here. Words and courage failed me. She brought her lips to mine, and we entwined.

"Right, well I need to get going. I promised Frank a date night. See you soon." My heart sank as she got up and got dressed. I could never compete with Frank. He was family to her. Not that I would ever compete with him. He was a blessing to Isabella's life. And in a few swift minutes, she kissed me goodbye and left. I rolled over and groaned my frustration in the shitty pillow.

The following day without her was agony. With little to do, I spent most of my time in my room, only leaving it to buy food and beer. I had no clue what to do but waited for Isabella to call. The solitary confinement of my room grew my impatience as I longed for my small apartment back in Devon. It wasn't much, but I was secure and accustomed to my routine. Surfing in the mornings, eating, reading and running on the beach in the evenings. In London, I was exposed to those I tried to leave in my past life. The people whom I couldn't let near Isabella. Hours passed, and I heard nothing, so I called her. No answer. I redialled her number and nothing. I figured she was busy with Frank or with the Nathan guy. I hoped that wasn't true. Then I received a call from an unknown number.

"So you're still lurking around on our turf. You have some nerve given that you owe us a lot of money."

"Clara. Still The Wolf's honorary secretary, I see." I knew I had hit a nerve when she paused for a moment.

"You should be a little nicer since we helped when you were nearly dying in that hotel room. You know, the time you got your arse handed to you by a woman." She laughed mockingly.

"What do you want?"

"A meeting. To discuss your misbehaviour, darling. We're not asking. I'll text you the address. Be there at midnight." The line went dead before I could respond. I redialled the number, but it was disconnected, although it was no surprise considering the people I was dealing with. Shit.

I thought about the first time I met them through Andrew. He was in all sorts of schemes to make money on the side. And as usual, I had to pick him up when he drank too much at a poker game after losing all his money to The Wolf's men. Fifteen thousand pounds, to be exact. I didn't have that kind of money to spare, nor did he after he lost his job over the Juliana situation, so I made a deal with these people to be their delivery guy a few times, and they would forget the debt.

On the other hand, Andrew had moved on to blackmailing Isabella while I ended up in a trap. Deliveries led to the safekeeping of their warehouses, and before I knew it, I was beating up men who refused to pay their debt also. Looking back, I wish I had taken my chances in a physical fight rather than be caught up in their trafficking and illicit games. These people knew everything about me and all my moves. Then they managed to lure Isabella into their den when they took me from her apartment. They didn't expect her to kill some of their established workers. I knew they wouldn't stop messing with her, so I diverted their attention back to me by running away. Sure, I could've told Isabella about this but knowing her so well, she would've run towards the danger and gotten herself killed. And these people didn't care if you were a man or woman. They killed anyone who got in their way. I, on the other hand, wanted no part in it. So I decided to stop and get out of this once and for all when we met.

Minutes later, an address popped up in a message on my phone. I knew exactly where it was from memory. It was a small warehouse hidden behind a deli in an industrial estate where I filled in for someone's shift. It was just a garage to the local public, but I knew what was hidden in the cars and vans. Illegal weapons and drugs. I paced my room, packing everything I needed for a quick getaway if I made it back that evening. I also tried to call Isabella to no avail.

Book Four

Chapter Six

Book Four

Ryan

I thought about going to her apartment but then thought that the people Clara worked for were probably following my every move to make sure I didn't try to run away. It was a possibility that they had eyes on us since I came back, but considering the courtesy phone call from Clara, I understood that I had their full attention. Minutes passed as I continued to pace around my room, trying to figure out what to do. Then realising that I didn't have to wait until midnight to meet The Wolf. I could go there right now with the element of surprise on my side. I wasn't sure what they wanted, but a hint of dread coursed through me. I swallowed and drowned my thoughts leaving only one that circled my mind. *I will kill for Isabella.* With that fuelling my adrenaline, I decided it was time to leave.

Isabella

The hours after I left Ryan's room dragged, but I wasn't scared. At least I convinced myself that I wasn't afraid of what I was about to do. Sure, I killed many people, one by accident and the others mostly out of self-defence, but this was like going into the dragon's pit. As always, making love to Ryan was intoxicating, and I didn't want to believe he was involved with The Wolf. I had managed to put a tracker on his phone while he slept. It was stupid for someone to not use a code these days. But fortunately for me, I was able to install and hide the app quickly while resisting the urge to snoop. I didn't ask him outright if he was involved with these people because I didn't want to trust his answer. I had to see it for myself. And now, as I looked down at my phone, watching his dot stuck to his room, I felt guilt build up in my stomach. Still, I was so deep in this mess, and I couldn't stop now. Even if I wanted to, it was not my nature to give up and cower in the darkness. I had to finish this, even if I ended up dead.

An hour later, I stirred on my sofa with my phone clenched in my hand. "Shit". I quickly swiped my screen to view the app and found that Ryan was on the move, further away from the bed and breakfast. That was my queue to follow him.

He's moving, and I'm right behind him. I'll send you my location.

I messaged Frank, grabbed my bag and made my way out of the door. I didn't have a plan or want to hurt anyone, but I had to see for myself and confirm the information Mik found. I thought I'd deal with the rest as they come. As my feet touched the pavement, I considered my next move; Ryan's dot was quite far, so I decided to hail a taxi and gave the driver directions. As we moved, the dot stopped, and it took me twenty minutes to get close. I paid the driver and climbed out of the car while looking over my shoulder to ensure nobody was watching. The dot lingered on a side street that looked like an industrial estate on my map. He stopped right behind a deli which was weird. There was no way he travelled this far for a sandwich. I quickly messaged Frank about the new location. This was it. I was going to confront him.

I walked in the direction of the dot on the app, and sure enough, there was a deli in the middle of the industrial estate. It was just after 7 p.m. when I checked the time, although there was nobody around, and the only visible light was from the deli that looked empty. *Weird.* The dot on the tracking app was idle and kept flashing as I moved closer. Still, Ryan was nowhere to be seen. I decided to keep a safe distance and walked around the back of the deli, where I heard his voice. He was talking to a woman, and her voice sounded familiar.

My heart pounded as jealousy began to creep into my veins. Their voices were low and intense until they moved further away into a small warehouse. I ducked behind a large recycling container and edged my head out to see them both standing by the warehouse entrance. The woman finished her cigarette, and they eventually went inside. My nostrils flared with anger, and I had to know more. So I carefully followed behind, staying low and quiet. Inside, the warehouse was larger than I expected, but fortunately, the place was dimly lit. I followed the faint sound of voices to a small office that had a surprisingly feminine touch. The scent of sandalwood and rose filled the air; the rest of the furniture was plush with luxurious velvet lining. Who were these people? Though the office was fully equipped to conduct business, it was empty. So I crept closer to the voices that had multiplied further inside the warehouse.

"You and Clara have to stay connected until it's done. You do this, and we let you go." A rough voice commanded. He sounded foreign. I could hear Ryan sigh and clear his throat. Mike was right. He was working with these people, and I suspected he was sleeping with Clara. Rage erupted, and I could feel my ears growing hot. Before I could stop myself, I could feel my feet moving towards them. It was such a stupid thing to do, but I couldn't stop.

"You prick!" I spat. There were two unknown men, Clara and Ryan, whose eyes narrowed in my direction with confusion and panic.

"Isabella. You shouldn't be here."

"Yes, Isabella, or should I call you Jayne Johnson?" Clara remarked as Ryan looked at her with silent fury and confusion. "Oh, didn't you know baby? Your girlfriend here paid me a visit. She almost caught me off guard but fortunately we're always a step ahead. Just how she managed to track us down is beyond me, a clever one she is." Clara smirked.

"She's not in this!" Ryan shouted.

"Oh, but I think you'd find that she is now. She killed John, Andrew and Detective Johnson. Although, that woman was already on thin ice with us" She grimaced, counting on her fingers. "And don't forget the others she killed while trying to save your arse. Although that was partly your fault, to be fair. So, you see, baby, she is very much in this." I hated her calling him baby, but I was trying to understand the situation. Clara did all the talking while the other men watched calmly. Who was this woman? Like the last time I saw her, she was well-dressed in a green pencil dress with her hair tied in a sleek ponytail. She looked older than me, but that could've been the makeup. Her slender body towered over me as her heels sparkled under the dim light. I hated to admit it, but she was beautiful. And I couldn't blame Ryan for wanting her. As though he had read my mind, he looked at me with a horrifying look.

"We are not together whatsoever! You must believe me Izzy."

"Awww, how cute. Baby's in love." Clara chuckled. This was not the woman I saw in her office a few days ago. This version of her was sinister, and an aura of darkness radiated around her. She stood with confidence that made me wonder if I had met my match. "So, what do you say, Ryan, are you in?"

The room fell silent for a beat that seemed to last forever as Ryan contemplated his next step. I didn't know what these men did or who they were, but I understood they weren't high street accountants. Their calmness was unusual, and it put me on edge. I looked around the room, weighing my option should things turn sour, but I couldn't see anything I could use as a weapon to protect myself.

"No." Ryan answered, and with that simple word, Clara and the two men drew out their guns. Shit. Fear and adrenaline rippled through me, but I realised that I could lose the love of my life in a heartbeat. These people didn't play games by the rules, nor did they waste their time making their point. I looked around and calculated my odds. It was three against two; I've had worse.

"Look. Clearly you trust him since you want him to see through whatever your demand was. And you know he trusts me. I'm assuming you've done your job and know what I'm capable of. So, if he won't do it, let me. Once it's done, we both walk free, and you won't ever hear from us again."

The room stayed silent for a moment until Clara sighed. "That could work." Just when I thought I managed to scrape our escape from death, a loud, sharp bang echoed in the room that was instantly followed by a searing pain that sent shockwaves through my leg. My mouth opened to scream, but nothing came out. My body buckled to the floor, and my vision was blurred with shock. I had heard stories from some of my clients, but the reality of being shot was much worse. My body trembled, still; like a snake with its tail cut off, I slid around, trying to stand up.

"Oh my god, Isabella!" Ryan's voice echoed around me as the two men held him back while Clara approached me. I stopped moving, knowing I wasn't going anywhere soon. My heart pounded as my mouth filled with bile. Ryan was still fighting his way out of the man's grip, and I knew that if that was my final moment, I would die with pride.

"You're a fucking bitch." I spat at Clara, who was now standing above me and looking down with a sneer. I looked straight up at her, letting her know I wasn't afraid of death. She bent down and stroked my hair.

"Shhhh let this be a warning that I don't play around. I know you're not afraid of death, but I will make sure yours is extremely painful if you or little baby over there decide to waste my time." She stood up and walked off, leaving the trail of her heels echoing in the warehouse. I was angry at Ryan for letting this escalate and for not telling me about the extent of this situation. Even with a bullet in my leg, I was still unsure what chaos he was involved in. Another scorching pain shot up my leg, and a silent whimper escaped my mouth.

"Look she said she'll do it, please, help her!" Ryan shouted at the men. Then it dawned on me that I agreed to do something without knowing what the task was. Then, everything went black.

I awoke to a beeping machine in a room resembling a hospital. Although, I knew that the chances of these people taking me to a hospital were highly unlikely. My mouth was dry, and my leg now had an ache dulled with Vicodin and whatever else they added to the IV. I wasn't surprised by the change in my determination but by how I leaned in so quickly to prevent them from shooting Ryan. And now my leg was paying the price. Nonetheless, we both had a job to finish.

I was stuck in that bed for a few days, only able to hobble to the bathroom on crutches. The doctor was undoubtedly a crook on The Wolf's payroll with a day job at a private hospital. He was middle-aged, tall, medium built with greying hair, and we would've dated if we weren't in this situation. Despite the nature of our acquaintance, he was gentle and kind. "The bullet came out in one piece, so healing shouldn't take long." He gave a curt nod. "You can get back to business soon." He left the room before I could respond. I saw him dial a number on his phone between the blinds and spoke quietly. No doubt he was reporting back to his employer.

When I let out an isolated sigh, Ryan walked in with a jug of water. "It's good to see your eyes are open." He tried to smile, but neither of us was on form. "Here make sure you stay hydrated." I turned my face to focus on the doctor, who was now checking his messages on his phone. "That was such a stupid fucking thing you did. Out of all the shit you've pulled, this is by far the worse Isabella." He advanced closer to my bed until his face was so close to mine that I felt the warmth of his breath. "You could've gotten yourself killed." At that moment, I saw his eyes glisten.

"I am aware of that! How about a thank you for saving your life?" This man really infuriated me.

He retreated into a chair and held my hand. "Izzy. Thank you for saving my life." He lightly stroked my hand with his thumb and gently kissed it. A kiss that sent a shiver up my spine. We sat silently for a while, with so many questions in my mind.

"What business did I agree to?"

Don't worry about that for now. Focus on getting your strength back."

"I can't believe that fucking bitch shot me." He stayed silent, but I knew that he was aware I wouldn't let it go. He could try to protect her, but I would have her head on a spike, given the chance.

"Why are you involved with these people Ryan?" The silence grew wider between us until the room felt heavy. Each breath felt like he was battling to open up and tell me the truth.

"Andrew." I shuddered when I heard his name. The man I had killed. His brother. "He was involved with these people, and as usual, I had to clean up his mess. I offered to do a job for them to clear his debt, and it just spiralled from there. They're the people who helped me out of that hotel room, they supplied the fake credit cards and IDs. That's why I had to leave. I wanted nothing to do with them anymore, and I didn't want them messing with you. So, I disappeared."

"It doesn't really matter now. They were going to mess with me anyway. I saw a picture of you with Clara online. I think she wanted me to see it. They know what I've done and what I'm capable of, it was only a matter of time before they got me." His head hung low, deep in thought. "Did you sleep with her?"

"Clara?". I didn't want to think I imagined it, but I swear I saw his face go pale.

"She calls you baby and I see the way she looks at you."

"Izzy, she calls everyone that and she's quite intense." At that moment, I jumped up as I remembered Frank.

"I texted Frank and told him to keep his distance. But your phone is in your bag in that cupboard over there." He responded as though he read my mind, although I noticed a hesitancy in his face and wondered if there was more to him and Clara than he was letting on. "Look, tomorrow is a new day, for now just rest and get your strength back. I'm glad we're both still alive." He said as our eyes clung to one another. I wanted to kiss him, but it wasn't worth aggravating the dull pain in my leg, especially when I was sceptical about him and Clara.

I should've felt stupid for volunteering myself the way I did, but Ryan and I were connected, and I wasn't ready to let him go. Besides, I certainly didn't expect little miss crazy to shoot me in the leg. I promised myself I would seek my revenge and make sure the bitch crawled before me, begging for her life once the job was done. Hours passed as Ryan and I steeped in silence. He fell asleep in the chair by my bed while I calculated every possible scenario that could unfold over the next few days. I wanted to call Frank, but it was best that he wasn't involved. Fortunately, my belongings were placed in a cupboard nearby, and I thought I would check my messages as soon as I had some privacy. My paranoia told me cameras were everywhere, and I knew they were watching everything. I must've fallen asleep, although I didn't know how long for; I opened my eyes to find the chair beside me empty.

Chapter Seven

Hearing her scream in pain was like someone had pierced a knife through my heart. I encountered a lot of emotional traumas in the past; even physical ones didn't come close to this pain. It felt worse as she volunteered herself to Clara to save my life. Again, it was a predicament that opened the door of shame. Isabella was strong and tenacious to a fault. Now, she was in bed, with sweat beads forming on her skin while her body healed her wound. I was reminded of how precious she was to me. The job she agreed to do wasn't the worst I've seen Clara coordinate, but I didn't want her involved with these people. They played dirty, and they would never let her go. We had to find a way out of this. When I returned to check on her, she was hobbling on crutches.

"What do you need?" She turned abruptly and stared at me with agitation.

"My phone, my bath, some fucking bourbon and that bitch dead." She said through gritted teeth. Stunned yet proud of her sudden determination, I dared to approach closer and rested my hands on her cheeks.

"Well this looks cosy." Clara's voice echoed from outside the room as her heels left a trail of clicks until she opened the door. "You've recovered well little kitty." She smirked. "Grab your things and follow me." Isabella and I looked at each other, and I proceeded to grab her bag from the drawer. I exited the room and prompted her to follow close behind.

Clara led us into a room that was much larger than her office. This room was more extravagant, with large leather sofas and low-hanging crystal chandeliers. The air was also different; it was lighter, and I soon realised that the work of the white walls made everything look clean. To the right of the room was a bar cart, and next to that, a desk and matching chair, with papers neatly piled on the top right corner. A pen holder close by and a laptop. This person was meticulous with their space. Like before, though, it was Clara, Isabella and me while the two men waited outside the door. I looked at Isabella in anticipation. Then, a voice broke into the silence.

"Welcome." Sure enough, it was The Wolf, dressed in a dapper suit with a fresh haircut. I hadn't officially met him, as all his coordinated dealings were done through Clara and his men. But I had seen him when he thought he was invisible. "I've been informed that you two have become quite a nuisance." He smirked while Clara lounged on the sofa. He walked to the bar cart and poured two tumblers of bourbon, handing one to Clara. They both sipped at the same time. The silence continued for a moment.

"Can I have some?" My heart raced as Isabella asked the question. The vein in my neck grew as I waited for something to happen. "I mean, you're quite rude. This bitch shot me in the leg after I volunteered to do the job. Sure, we're not on social rapport but here you are holding us captive dressed like a gentleman yet, you're not upholding the gentleman etiquette." He raised an eyebrow and broke into a small laugh. Then, he walked over to the bar cart and poured her a drink.

Isabella

I didn't have a plan to get out of this, so I thought I'd challenge him to see how pliable his character was. When I asked for a drink, I knew he would relent or kill me, but he didn't dress like he liked to get his hands dirty. And the two idiots outside the door were hardly paying attention. I was in no condition to get into a physical fight, so it was a relief when he relented and poured me a serving of bourbon. Meanwhile, Clara continued to lounge on the sofa, looking bored. It took everything in me to not smack the shit out of her for what she did to me, but I knew I'd be dead in a second if I moved on The Wolf's favourite warrior. I made a mental vow that I would get her eventually like I had all the ones before. The silence lingered for a while before The Wolf said anything.

"I trust the bourbon is to your liking?" I nodded and thanked him as the burn of the spirit traced my chest, and the subtle high elevated my mind. I was ready to talk business. "By now, I'm sure you know that I'm The Wolf and I run this organisation." I wasn't sure if he was expecting applause, but I refused to stroke his ego. Especially since I wasn't sure to what extent he knew about me and my 'friends'. Perhaps he was aware of Frank but not Mik and his guys. They were meticulous and extremely private with their work, and that thought alone reassured my anxiety. Clara shifted on the sofa, and her distant sigh pulled me out of my thoughts.

"So what's the job?" He held my gaze for a moment before breaking into a smirk.

"I'm starting to like you." He pointed playfully. But I knew not to let my guard down. "You and Ryan will go on a road trip to the Lake District. I'm sure you're familiar with the place." It had been months since the incident in the Lake District. The memories of John and his twisted games, how I'd thought I killed Ryan. It was much simpler back then when I knew how to separate my emotions and logic. Now, I was fighting for us both to survive these people. "You will meet with a man called Tate. He's our contact from the States, and you will collect a parcel and bring it back here safely. The job is simple: no games and no drama. You complete the task, and we let you both go."

I knew for a long time that nothing was ever simple. I killed in self-dense and out of ego, Frank killed by accident, and Ryan, from what I knew, had never taken someone's life. Yet, here we all were, one way or another, caught in the wolf's entanglement.

A few hours later, Ryan and I walked into my apartment. Frank had relocated Jules to his apartment to look after him, and I felt a slight weight lifted from my shoulders, knowing that the kitten was safe and living in comfort during my absence. I called him to explain that I would be out of the city for a while but decided to keep some of the details from him just in case Clara had put a tracker on my phone. Regardless,

I trusted Frank would know what to do if I was ever in trouble. I just hoped he would do the right thing this time and leave this city and the mess behind to start a new life. As I stood deep in thought in my beautiful kitchen, the dull ache in my leg jolted me back to reality. I winced and slowly walked to the sofa.

"Here, take these. It should kick in quickly." Ryan handed me a Vicodin with a glass of water, but I slowly stood up and headed to the small corner bar for a small serving of bourbon, knowing just how badly I needed to numb the physical and emotional pain. He stood and stared at me for a moment.

"I don't need your judgement right now. I've been on one hell of a ride." I hobbled back to the sofa.

"You should eat something. I'll make you some lunch." It was closer to dinner time than lunch, and the last thing I wanted was food. I longed for my freedom now more than ever. We were instructed to leave the following evening in a rental car. Naturally, I would be in the passenger's seat since I couldn't drive in my condition. This was the more reason I yearned for control. I told myself we would keep our heads down and finish the job, but my intuition knew it wouldn't be that simple. Ryan and I were magnets for trouble.

Thirty minutes later, my pain was non-existent as my mind faded in the low hum of the fridge that filled the silence of my apartment. Ryan hadn't spoken much, and our conversation had faltered to a mute, which was fine with me since I just wanted to enjoy the numbness of the Vicodin until I succumbed to sleep.

The following morning, I awoke with a fog that only a strong coffee could pull me through. I slowly went through my apartment, ensuring everything was in place while Ryan slept on the sofa. In the shower, I let the heavy water beads beat the tension out of my skin. It felt like a reprieve. My hair reverted into its tight curls, with my blond highlights now dulled in black. I felt achy and icky, as though I couldn't get my skin clean enough. Being in that warehouse makeshift hospital room was horrendous, and I was grateful to be in the comfort of my own home. Although the thought of returning to that hotel in the lake district was unnerving, I would still slap on my business mask and power through just like I had done over the past months.

I took my time in the bathroom and decided to sleek my hair back into a messy bun. Buns weren't my go-to style, but at this point, it was easier to go for the clean girl look. I kept my makeup minimal to not draw any unwanted attention to myself. I walked meticulously to my bedroom and opted to wear something casual that was easy to get into. And since I had a bulky bandage on my leg, I thought a pair of loose-fitting trousers and a chic grey jumper would suffice. I packed my overnight bag and my emergency folder. This would stay extremely close to me in case I needed to flee.

I thought Frank would know what to do with the rest of my things if I needed to leave the country quickly. We had already worked out a plan should we ever need to leave together; however, I trusted that he would know what to do if he had to leave alone. My mind faded into my thoughts as I packed my items, and I suddenly doubled over with the realisation of who Clara was. I wondered why she looked so familiar since I first saw her face, but the bullet in my leg had stolen my focus. And now it was clear that she was the same woman I saw Nathan on a date with a few days after I had met him. This city was getting really small, and I knew it was time for me to move on when all of this was done. My heart raced at the epiphany, but I kept calm. But then I wondered if Nathan was somehow involved with The Wolf's organisation. Was he officially the events manager or caterer? I frowned in confusion. Detective Johnson was right. The hole and web of lies grew deeper.

Ryan

I awoke after a restful sleep on Isabella's sofa. It had been my best sleep since being stuck in that warehouse, and I was determined to have an indulgent breakfast, lunch and dinner before we got the rental car and headed on the road. Clara booked the rental car to meet us in the evening to minimise drawing attention to us or perhaps to be dramatic. Regardless, I aimed to finish this job and leave this city, preferably taking Isabella. I cooked a full English breakfast while listening to Isabella's humming in the bathroom. I couldn't tell if she was in a better mood than the night before or if she was nervous. It wasn't until I walked to her bedroom and announced that breakfast was ready that I saw her pacing around her room, packing a bag. I knew she would bring her closest luxuries for comfort, but something was off. Especially when she jumped as though she had forgotten I was in her apartment.

"Are you okay?"

"Erm, yeah, just making sure I have everything I need." She hesitated before she pull herself together.

"Well, breakfast is ready." I took my time to study her and waited for her to follow behind as we headed into the living room, where I had set the coffee table with our Full English and fresh juice.

"This looks lovely. Thank you." She forced a smile, although I genuinely thought she meant the compliment.

We ate in silence and exchanged the odd teasing glances with one another. I didn't know what would happen over the next few hours, but I could predict we would bicker and make up quickly. That's just what we did. When we finished breakfast, I went through the cleaning and tidying up routine while Isabella nursed her cup of coffee with her foot elevated on the sofa. I knew that she was either anxious or in pain.

"I wish I could go for a run to burn some energy. I hate just sitting here waiting on the impending doom."

"This is so boring."

"Why don't you go and see Frank. It's been a while. I can come with you, make sure you get there safe and meet you afterwards."

She contemplated for a moment, then agreed. "Fine, but you don't have to come with me. I'll call you if I need you."

And with that, she finished her coffee, grabbed her purse and left.

Isabella

Every second spent waiting to leave felt like I was drowning in a muddy lake. I did nothing but think about Clara's relationship with Ryan, but most of all, I was thinking about Frank. I wondered whether it was a good idea to call him since I'd been home or whether it would be better to go to his apartment. I felt like I was constantly being watched, and even when I knew that Ryan was on my side, I still felt like the current situation had strained our relationship. I needed space to think things through without him hovering around my apartment. I was independent and loved to do things my way, on my own time. I couldn't have left fast enough when he suggested I visit Frank. So, I made my way to his apartment as fast as the bandage on my leg, and the crutches I relied on would allow. I was exhausted and out of breath when I reached Frank's floor.

"What the fuck happened Izzy?" Frank demanded as he opened the door to find me looking flustered and sweaty.

"That fucking bitch shot me, that's what happened." I went to his bedroom, rested the crutches by the door and made myself comfortable on his bed. "God I've missed this bed." I took a deep breath as Frank sat next to me. Ryan had texted him about the situation, but it had been a few days since I saw or spoke to Frank. I had a lot to tell him.

"Wow, that was a ballsy move, but don't do that again. I don't know how I could live my life without you, if she had aimed for your head." We fell silent as the thought of what could've been grew more vivid.

"Anyway, I think I can do this Frank. I just need to get through this arrangement, pick up the package and drive back. Then I want to get the fuck out of here. For good. Maybe we can go to Paris or Venice?" He hesitated.

"I was thinking about this Izzy and I'm really happy here, with Mik. I finally have some stability and as close to a normal relationship as I could get with the kind of lives we live. I told you before, I would do anything for you. Is there a way we can make it work here? Maybe we can move further south like Ryan did?"

I couldn't say that I was surprised. I knew and saw Frank's happiness since he got with Mik. He was more grounded and logical, less spoiled. And I promised myself that I would never take that from him or make him choose me over Mik. That's why I had emotionally prepared myself for when he admitted that this was what he wanted and needed.

"Babe, I can't stay here anymore with a target on my back. I need to be able to breathe and sleep at night. I love you and Mik so much and I will never suggest you do anything other than follow your heart."

"So this is the end of our friendship? You leave and I stay here, I can't lose you Izzy." His eyes glistened with tears.

"Hey, there will never be an end to our friendship. Stop that." I cupped his cheek, looking ridiculous as always since he was four times my size. His cheek was sleek and chiselled as usual, but the comforting warmth that his body exuded made me feel safe. "Just because I'm choosing to leave England doesn't mean we'll never see each other again. We'll visit and see each other when I've settled in somewhere. And I can see that Jules have settled in here with you, so it's only fair for you to keep him. You are so much more nurturing to him than I ever was. We're family, and that will never change. I just need some time away from here and relax."

"You're right." He smirked. "Jules and I make such a great team." And just like that, my mood elevated as I looked forward to my freedom.

Outside, the cold air blew while the noisy city sang in its eventful schedules. Cars and ambulances drove by while the kids played in the nearby park. Just like the hustle and bustle of this crazy city, Frank and I had been on a rollercoaster ride to hell and back. However, in the past few weeks, I decided to return to tie up some loose ends, only to end up with a noose around my neck. A new beginning was on my horizon, and I decided to keep it to myself for a while. I guessed that Ryan would choose to stay in this country once everything was done, and I couldn't let him convince me to stay here with him. My love affair with this city was over, and so was my thirst for constant luxury and financial promiscuity. Although, I hoped that I, too, could have what Frank and Mik had. I sighed in the frenzy of my thoughts. So, Frank opened his bedside drawer and pulled out a joint, which we shared until I returned home.

Chapter Eight

Book Four

Isabella

It was after late lunchtime when I arrived home. Ryan had ordered food. My mouth was dry, and my stomach rumbled when the smell of my favourite takeaway lingered in the kitchen.

"Pizza!". I tried to skip towards the kitchen but was quickly humbled by my healing leg.

"Be careful! You're becoming careless with that leg. The pizza's not going anywhere, so take it easy."

"I'm independent Ryan, always have been and always will be. Get over it." I half teased as I opened the box and inhaled the aroma.

"I take it you had fun with Frank?" He knew I was buzzed, and I couldn't care less if he had a slight critique on this.

"I sure did." I said mid-chew. "Only a few more hours before the car gets here, so I'll finish this and have myself a little catnap." He smiled and shook his head. This light playfulness was effortless, and I wished we could've stayed like that for a while. My heart turned slightly cold when I realised that I had to tell him about my decision to leave when this was over. However, in the meantime, I finished eating my pizza, cleaned myself up and indulged in an afternoon nap.

By the time I awoke from my nap, it was early evening. A slight chill had settled at the base of my spine with the realisation that it was time to get on the road. Ryan was pacing around the apartment, ensuring he had everything in his bags. I headed for a quick shower to rinse off the residue of my buzz. It took no more than ten minutes before I was dressed and ready to go.

"So, what's happening with your things at the B&B?" I asked as it had been lingering on my mind.

"I didn't bring much. I went back earlier while you slept to grab my clothes, passport and cash. Everything else were just instant noodles and cheap shower gels. The car's here."

And with that, we went downstairs for our little road trip. The rental car that Clara sent was nice, and I was surprised to see that The Wolf hadn't been stingy with the expense. Everything was new and clean, and the Satellite Navigation system was seamless. This took the pressure off as Ryan could focus on the driving whilst I focused on getting my head in the game and planning my way out once this was done. However, somewhere along the journey, I fell asleep and woke up in the darkness with the flicker of oncoming headlights. Ryan's eyes were glued to the road ahead with his arms stretched out, guiding the steering wheel with ease. In moments like this, I saw him in his magnificence.

"How long have we been driving?"

"About an hour and a half. Do you need to stop to stretch your legs?" He gently placed his left hand on my thigh.

"No, I'm okay. Do you?" I glanced over at him.

"This isn't my first time doing this. I can go a few hours without stopping." He smirked, and I immediately knew he was being cheeky.

We continued with the small talk for a while.
"What was your first thought when you saw me for the first time?" I couldn't believe he wanted to go back there, but I was never one to squirm under pressure.

"Fuck he is hot!" I laughed as he looked over at me and back to the road in disbelief. "What? It's true. I thought you were really hot actually." We fell in silence for a moment. "And you, what was your first thought of me?" Something shifted on his face, but I kept my focus on him. After a long silence, he answered.

"I thought that you were the most beautiful woman I had ever seen. Powerful, in a divine way from how you carried yourself. Then, after we first slept together, I thought that I wanted you to be mine forever."

"Wow." I was speechless. Of course, I had heard men say things like that to me, which was why they paid to be with me, but the way Ryan said it left me speechless. We continued to drive silently while I decided to break into the snack supplies and share a packet of crisps. Hours passed before it was time to stop and stretch our legs. The pain in my healing wound was nothing more than an annoying dull ache. Still, hatred continued to brew from inside as my heart paced, waiting to take my revenge on Clara.

Ryan

We arrived at the Lake District just after midnight. The hotel was located only a few minutes from Lake Windermere. Unsurprisingly, checking into our room was swift and seamless, as I knew Clara was exceptional at coordinating in her role. Being The Wolf's right hand meant she had to be efficient and one step ahead. The suite was on the second floor at the far end of the corridor. Isabella had fallen asleep with her neck at an angle in the car, and I could feel her agitation as she tried to rub the tension out of her muscles. Since we didn't have to meet the connection until the morning, I asked the front desk to send a masseuse while Isabella freshened up in the bathroom. It took us twenty minutes to get settled into the room. As I contemplated our dinner plans, the masseuse arrived with a bed ready to have Isabella back to her calm self.

I made myself busy, studying the menu and flipping through the documents on the other side of the suite while the faint sound of crashing waves and aromatherapy oils poured from the other side of the room. We weren't told what we were transporting back to London. However, I guessed that it wasn't legal. My best guess was drugs or dirty money. The Wolf had better means to transport firearms and whatever he fancied. Forty-five minutes passed when I heard Isabella express her gratitude to the masseuse, and the suite door closed.

"Feeling better?" She lazily walked towards me.

"Yes, thanks for booking that. I'm ready to eat and relax."

"Okay, I'll order. Should be here by the time you finish having a shower." And with that, I dialled for room service and ordered two club sandwiches and some juice. The food arrived just as quickly as Isabella emerged from the bathroom. We ate in a silence that filled the room, yet my mind pounded with thoughts from our earlier conversations. The car ride wasn't as terrible as I expected, although I never let my frustration with this situation show to not tip Isabella over the edge. But truth be told, I was terrified of losing her. I was nervous about what could happen here, in the place where my life fell apart for good. I filled myself with hope that we could make a home out of this darkness together. Besides, I had decided that she was the love of my life after all.

I don't know what time we fell asleep, but I awoke with the sound of Isabella's hair dryer and a dull tension that radiated through my neck. I felt as though I barely slept. I had no choice but to push through the day. The Wolf's Connect confirmed the meeting for 11 a.m., so we had enough time to order breakfast and mentally prepare. Clara had insisted on regular check-ins, and the more I ignored her calls, the louder her voice became on the ones I did accept. Isabella knew I was supposed to check in with 'the bosses,' but I tried to keep these calls brief and as quiet as possible. She was thirsty for revenge, and I needed the day to go as planned.

"So, we're not hanging around. He'll want to make small talk when he sees you so keep it light and brief. Once the package is in our hands, we check out and leave." She nodded in agreement. I sensed a weird nervousness that lingered between us. "Hey, it's going to be fine. We've been through worse." She nodded again.

The connection insisted on meeting at the bar, and finding him wasn't difficult. He was dressed in standard business attire, but like everyone involved with The Wolf, he stood with an edge. After a beat of scrutiny, I realised he had no bag or anything indicating a package to be transported back with us. I instantly knew his game. I lightly tapped Isabella on the small of her back, and like an unspoken secret language, she raised an eyebrow in understanding. We approached the man until we got close enough for him to see us. "Afternoon." He said with a smirk as he saw Isabella and put out his hand. She gave her most charming smile and shook his hand. My possessive streak was ready to unravel, but I held onto my cool because this had to go well. "The package?" I stated rather than asked.

He took an edgy inhale before he answered in a half-whisper. "In my suite. Why don't you both come up for a drink, and we can conduct business in private." He also stated rather than asked. Isabella and I exchanged glances, then nodded in agreement. I saw the flames in her eyes dance with excitement. If this idiot tried something, she was ready to deal with him, and I, the lovesick Pit Bull that I was, would be happy to help her. The lift ascended to the fifth floor and opened to a solitary door that led to his suite. I didn't expect any less for a chap like him. He walked slowly and confidently to his mini bar and poured us three whiskey tumblers. We clinked our glasses and took a sip.

After a short pause, he spoke. "My name is Martin." His mouth curved into a phoney smile. We both obliged him but remained silent. He broke our stare, placed his glass on a small end table and walked to his sitting room to admire the panoramic view. "I like coming here, it's always tranquil and uneventful." With a swift move, I dropped a quick dissolvable tablet in his drink, and Isabella took the queue to join him.

"The package?" She interrupted.

"Your employer owes me so many favours and I don't want to give it to you without a little mischief." He grunted.

"And what do you have in mind?" She smirked.

"Well, I assume you don't want to go back empty-handed, so how about you have a late lunch with me." My back stiffened, knowing precisely what the slug was after.

"Okay. But I want to finish my drink first." She gave me a nod, and with a wary glare, I exited.

Isabella

I had to hold my composure so tightly that my stomach hurt. This poor excuse for a man had no idea who he was trying to play with. Ryan and I had already discussed a plan if things didn't go smoothly. Fortunately, this plan naturally unravelled in our favour when Martin invited us back to his suite. After Ryan left, he returned to the end table and picked up his drink. Then, he sat on the sofa, beckoning me to join him.

"How long have you been coming here for?" I fluttered my eyelashes and pretended to take a small sip of my drink. He didn't seem to notice that I had barely drunk it, and even if he did, his eyes didn't show that he cared as they lingered along the length of my body.

"A few times a year. How many times do you travel up here?" I watched him, longing for his lips to touch the drink in his hand.

"Just this once." I smiled. "So is there anything you would like to do for the rest of the afternoon?" He glared at his watch and said, "You."

"I think you got the wrong impression of me. I'll happily have lunch with you but I won't sleep with you."

"I never said anything about sleeping. Besides, I find the art of seduction much more fun than the action itself. So why don't you entertain me for a bit?" The nerve of this man. His arrogance was unappetising, and his sweat patch was repulsive.

"You can't really enjoy the seduction without some fun juice." I moved closer, arched my back and took the glass from his hand. "Drink up." I slowly poured the whisky into his mouth as I bit my bottom lip. Once the glass was drained, I seductively licked my lips, put the glass on the table, stood up and took off my top. I slowly gyrated my hips as his eyes twinkled with delight.

"You're really good at that." He slurred, then coughed. "Excuse me." He coughed again as I continued to move. "My throat is tickly, I think I need some water." This time, he coughed uncontrollably.

"Water won't do anything for you Martin. Just let it wash over you. It'll be less painful this way." His eyes glared at my face with shock.

"You bitch!" He tried to stand up, but his body became heavy, and his cough continued into a sudden gasp. That was his last breath. I had gotten used to seeing people die, and I had seen my fair share, but this one wasn't as satisfying as the rest. Martin was a predator, but he was pathetically stupid. When his eyes went blank, I put my top back on and looked around the room for the package.

Come back.

Ryan was back within a few minutes with a look of apprehension and irritation.

"Fuck. Did he touch you?"
"I didn't give him the chance to." He nodded with relief. I handed him a bag. I assumed he would want to see the contents for himself. He opened it and took out a heavy block tightly wrapped in plastic.

"Drugs, for sure. Judging by the weight I would say it's worth about 500K." My eyes widened. And knowing what kind of business The Wolf runs, it's most likely cocaine.

"So, we keep it for ourselves and sell it."

"Are you out of you mind? We've done some fucked up shit Izzy, but we're not drug dealers. I want no part in this plan. I just want my freedom." As much as I hated it, he was right. I had enough money saved to start over somewhere new, and if I made it back to my apartment in one piece, I had some gold bars and mined digital currencies on my hard drive. Selling cocaine would take too much time and effort.

"Fine. We bring it back to those lunatics and hope for the best? Even though you know they won't ever let us leave like that." His eyes lowered to my lips as he grabbed my shoulders.

"I know that but we're not wasting time selling drugs. Everything we've done up until now was out of necessity for survival, yes there were some collateral damages along the way, but we're here. Just us and we can make a choice to leave this shit behind and live our lives somewhere quiet by the beach or something." My heart felt heavy with the realisation that I needed to tell him I wanted to leave the country for good.

"That sounds lovely, but I've decided that I'm leaving the country. I can't stay here anymore. It's getting too much."

Book Four

Chapter Nine

Book Four

Ryan

The air froze between us, and all I could hear was the dull pulsing of my heart as I held onto my breath. The heaviness was the only thing keeping me alert as her words, once again, stabbed my heart mercilessly. All hopes I had of us building a different life together crumbled like a piece of scrap paper.

"And I suppose you've thought about this for a while?" She nodded. "You were never going to tell me?"

"I was waiting for the right time."

"Look around you Isabella, there is never a right time! Fuck. Why do you keep running from me?"

"This isn't about you! I'm tired of looking over my shoulder every time I leave the house. I'm tired of the anxiety that someone will kill me in my sleep or worse, going to jail. I need to get the fuck out of this country and I'm never coming back." She held her gaze just as firmly as she held her cards to her chest. And just as I was about to speak, my phone rang.

"Do you have the package?"

"Well good afternoon to you too Clara." Isabella rolled her eyes. "We have the package but there's a slight complication." I hesitated as she sighed down the phone. "He was playing hard to get and we won. He's dead." There was a long pause before Clara spoke.

"This is not how I like to conduct business Ryan. Nonetheless, we need the delivery by tomorrow evening at the latest. Get your things and be on your way." She spat.

"And the body?"

"We'll take care of it." The line went dead before I could ask further questions.

"What now?"

"We check out and get back to London. Given the traffic last night, I think we should give ourselves as much time as possible."

"Fine. But not without eating first or I'll get whiny." She smirked.

We finally scanned the suite and went to our room to pack and check out.

Checking out was swift, and even though a part of me bathed in anxiety about the dead body we had left behind, I trusted that Clara and her team knew just how to take care of the situation. This was reaffirmed by the memory of my past when they helped me escape death and prison because of Isabella's wrath. Still, I was back in the familiar place, only this time, my heart laid in her palm to be crushed for good. I also thought about how they would take care of us once we delivered the package. That was the most crucial question that swirled in my thoughts. My body ached with the tension and lack of sleep. It had only been a few hours since we left London, and with only a few hours to rest, my need to go to the gym and hit the punching bag was growing. However, Isabella was right that we should eat before returning to the city. Fortunately, we only brought a small bag each, and the package fitted snuggly at the bottom of mine. Ten minutes later, we were parked in a local Italian restaurant.

"This place is nice." Isabella said as she fidgeted with her ring.

"How's your leg?"

"Fine. But the scar isn't." She said as she gazed into the distance.

"You're going to be fine. It'll fade." I really wanted to say that the scar and this life will fade along with her memories of me. So, have you thought about where you'll go after this?"

The silence grew thick, and thankfully, the waiter arrived to take our order. After we started picking at our food and sipping our drinks, she decided to respond.

"I was thinking somewhere hot. The Bahamas or Seychelles."

"And far, it seems. When do you plan on leaving?"

"In a couple of weeks."

Isabella

The rest of our lunch was uneventful. We engaged in idle chatter as though the heaviness of the past occurrence were non-existent. Soon, though, it was time to drive back to London and face our future. This time, the traffic had us clenched between cars, and the motorway was as endless as the silence between us. We arrived in London just after 6 p.m., and the buzz of the busy streets elevated the thud in my head. The memory of the previous days flooded my mind as we parked the car on the private street parking outside of my apartment. The only comfort I felt was that I no longer needed to use a crutch to walk as the wound on my leg was healed. The scar, on the other hand, was destructive motivation. And I was a volcano waiting to erupt. My heartbeat matched each step I took to my home, and as we entered, I took a deep breath to take in the beauty of my décor. The luxury items I had bought sparkled in every corner. I had vowed against attachment to material items many years ago; that way, packing up and leaving would be easy, although I had slowly strayed from my vow. I had grown to love my home and everything in it. As Ryan set down our bags, I roamed to the kitchen and traced my hand along the granite countertops, remembering the fun memories of Frank and I cooking together, the first time we brought the kitten home and had no clue how to look after it, but my most haunting memory was the first time Ryan and I made love in there. That was the time I knew that I loved him. As though he sensed my nostalgia, he walked over and hugged me from behind, kissed my neck and almost growled in my ears.

"I remember that time too." His hands roamed my shoulders and traced to my navel until his fingers slipped under my top and worked their way to my chest. "I remember the first time you took my heart and made me eat out of your palm. You made me hard just standing there naked with a twinkle in your eyes in this kitchen. Just like now."

He continued to feel my breasts and kiss my neck, but this time, I turned around, and his mouth met mine. The air froze, and my only breath to survive was his. Our kiss grew intense, and we slowly walked to my bedroom.

"Take off your top." I commanded.

"Okay, Miss Bossy." He teased. He slowly stripped off his t-shirt, and soon his jeans followed, his muscles exposed to appease my desire. He slowly walked towards me and cupped my cheeks in his hands. I had always prevented men from doing this. Looking deep into my eyes was a forbidden act. They say the eyes are the windows to the soul, and my soul was dark; it was filled with death and all the other souls I had taken now resided in my darkness. But with Ryan, though, I wanted him to dive deep into my eyes as I bathed in his. But when he leaned in to kiss me deeper, I knew I couldn't keep the secrets any longer. Frank would've disapproved of this, but I had to tell him.

"Where did you go?" Ryan pulled back and searched my eyes.

"Look I want you more than you know but I can't carry on like this. I have so many secrets Ryan. And if you knew who I really am, you wouldn't want anything to do with me."

He withdrew and sat on the bed. "Try me." He shot a daring look.

"I've killed so many people." He stayed silent but raised an eyebrow to say he was not surprised. "When I was sixteen, I killed my stepdad. He was abusive to my mother, and I woke up in the middle of the night to find him hitting and strangling her." I was unravelling, and so was my rambling. "I hit him on the head with a baseball bat, cleaned it up, and the police thought his death was caused by a stab wound that my mother gave him before he killed her. I was then moved to a foster home without suspicions, and I got away with it."

He puffed out air and glared at me momentarily before speaking. "So, you tried to help your mother against her abuser and killed him." I nodded. "I would've done the same or worse, to be honest. That's not going to push me away, Isabella."

"Okay, in my first year in London, a woman was trying to bully me in Pilates, so I slipped some pills in her water and she died. I have trail of deaths in this city, including Andrew and John. And a few months ago, Frank and I met a man in a club, he came back here the next day and was forceful after I rejected him. He tried to assault me so I killed him, in self-defence." I chewed on my lip and stayed silent.

"Carry on." He prompted as the veins on his neck grew.

"And just after that, the detective who came here to investigate Mike's disappearance threatened Frank. We broke into her house to investigate her with the help of Frank's guys, and I found out that she was corrupted, worked for The Wolf and facilitated his trafficking. Her and her colleagues were involved with The Wolf, they blackmail and hurt people. She had hundreds of pictures and documents on Frank, me and you. So, I killed her to get closer to The Wolf. At first I started to feel bad but after seeing the state of her house, she had a drug problem and malnourished kitten, so I took the kitten home and he now lives with Frank."

"Is that all?" He was still sat on the bed, rigidly waiting."

"And my real job…I'm not an interior design blogger or whatever I told you. I'm an escort. Or rather I used to be until a few weeks ago." This part did start to hurt when his face dropped, and his eyes shut. However, he stood and slowly walked toward me.

"I already knew all of this." Stunned. That was the only word to describe how I felt. "I knew everything about you after the day we fucked in my flat. Even after I left, I always had the resources to watch you. And when I wasn't watching you, I was reading your files from the foster care system. You're right about The Wolf. I told you I was working for him, and as much as I hated it, I got close enough to convince Clara to show me everything he had on you and Frank. I know you're trying to push me away, to make it easier for you to leave after this is done, but I'm not leaving you that easily.

Ryan

I fought an internal smile when her mouth drew wide after my revelation. Isabella was one hell of a woman, but I was a guardian of hell. I knew exactly what I was getting myself into when I succumbed to her seduction. It was unorthodox to those stuck living in the mundane, but our lives were far from mundane. I *knew* that she wasn't innocent, and neither was I. I had killed many people, too, and broke a few hearts until I first saw Isabella. That was when I knew I wanted to do and be better. And as for her profession, I knew exactly who she was sleeping with and taking money from. Female seduction was the most powerful force in the world, and Isabella was mighty. Bewitching. And I also knew that she had dwindled in her work since we reconnected. That's how I knew how much she wanted to be with me. Still, regardless of what we both encountered on the journey, I knew that our souls were meant to meet and be together in this lifetime.

"Baby, you don't need to explain anything to me. I know about it all. And the bits that I don't know don't matter now. Just tell me you'll stay with me." Tears flowed down her face with shock and relief. I kissed her hard and prompted her to the bed. She slowly undressed and climbed over me, grinding her hips on my manhood. A moment later, I climbed on top of her, kissed her neck and made my way down, eventually stopping between her thighs. She tasted just as I remembered. Magical. I continued to pleasure her there until small moans escaped her lips. I kissed my way back up to her neck and sucked on her bottom lip. She leaned into it, then pulled us closer and guided me to enter her. We fucked like the world was ending, and if the neighbours were in, I'd be surprised if they weren't listening through the walls. An hour later, we were both sitting naked on her bed, sharing a tumbler of bourbon.

I couldn't help but laugh. "What?"

"Sharing a glass of bourbon is what you usually do with Frank. Yet here we are." She smiled in contemplation.

"True, but Frank and I never fucked. Besides, we always shared a joint too."

"Alright it's not a competition but if it was, right now I'd be winning."

We both smiled because we knew that it was true. Frank was her family, and I would never get in between them, but what Isabella had just shared was another level of intimacy that I knew she would never share with anyone else. As I sat deep in thought, running my fingers through her curls, the clock on the far wall of her bedroom caught my attention. "We need to get going." There it was, the melancholy look on her face. "This has to be done Isabella, no matter what happens, I promise I'll protect you."

Twenty minutes later, we showered, ate and changed into casual clothes. Isabella went through her safe and started packing a small bag. My heart dropped as I realised what she was doing. She was packing her emergency getaway bag. She stopped when she saw me staring at her and walked over to bury her face in my neck.

"I'll stay with you Ryan. I want to stay with you because I'm madly in love with you. But I can't stay in this country anymore. It's too much." I closed my eyes in relief.

"I'll go anywhere you want me to baby. As long as I'm with you."

The journey back to the warehouse was silent. We had explored every scenario before we left the apartment. Still, we both knew that The Wolf played dirty, and Clara was his loyal servant. One nod from him, she wouldn't hesitate to pull the trigger and kill us herself. The edge we had was Isabella's fury and my determination to protect her and be free at all costs. I parked the car, and we walked inside with the package firmly in my grip. I gave Isabella a look of reassurance before we walked inside. Clara greeted us with a stern look. She stood tall and lean, wearing a bright green suit and satin beige blouse. Her hair was sleeked back, and her eyes sparkled under the fluorescent lights of the warehouse. If we didn't know any better, we would have thought she was the fashion stylist she officially claimed to be. But it was all smoke and mirrors, sham arrangements to launder The Wolf's dirty money and keep a low profile.

"The package." She held out her hand, and I handed it to her. "I didn't care much for the mess you made." I nodded.

"Okay, so you have what you asked for, we delivered it on time. I think we're done here." Isabella retorted. Part of me really wanted this to be the end. I had hoped she would agree to let us go, but I had been working for these people for years and knew this wasn't her decision to make.

Chapter Ten

Isabella

The nerve on this bitch. She stood there with a sinister smirk, begging for a punch, but I knew I had to keep my cool. Ryan gave her the package, and I thought I'd test the situation to see if she would let us leave. Ryan had warned that letting us leave that warehouse alive would be impossible because these people never played fair. The only way to be free was to take the freedom by force.

"Okay, so you have what you requested, we delivered it on time. I think we're done here." I spoke. Clara stood still momentarily before turning her back and motioning us to follow her to her office. She had two unfamiliar men with her this time, and they moved in sync. The clicking of her heels echoed throughout the room, and I found myself watching her intently. She was beautiful, and she smelled terrific. That uneasy feeling twisted in my stomach as I thought, how could a man like Ryan not want her. Hell, if I was a man, she would've been mine. Ryan grabbed my hand to pull my focus back to the situation.

"Have a seat." She motioned towards the plush sofa next to the bar in her office. We did as we were told. "Your request is not my decision to make and as much as I would like you out of my way, The Wolf however, needs you to complete one more job." She stood with her heels firmly planted on the ground. I took a moment to scrutinise her form. She fascinated me; perhaps we could've been friends in another life.

"No". Ryan stated. "We are done. You may be happy to spend your life being a servant to that madman, but this is not the life I want to-.

The Wolf walked into the office just as he was about to stand. "The life you want to what, Ryan?" He prompted.

"This is not the life I want to live and neither does Isabella."

The Wolf sighed. "This isn't the life any of us wanted boy, but shit happened, and we had to make do with the hands we were dealt. Let's not forget who brought you here. It wasn't me and certainly not Clara." He pointed to Clara. "You brought yourself here and begged me to show your brother mercy by volunteering yourself for the job." We stayed silent, and my heart thump wasn't strong enough to break the tension.

The Wolf walked to the bar and poured himself a drink. "Would you like some Isabella?" I shook my head to refuse because I was paralysed on the sofa. He grinned.

"As I was saying, you brought yourself to me and knew the cost. I told you, once you're in, there's no way out. Your brother Andrew knew this too. How is he by the way?" He smirked.

"He's dead." Ryan said deadpan.

"Of course, I knew that. I have eyes everywhere. And see, even when you sacrificed your life for him, he still ended up wasting his and dying anyway." He sipped his drink as we steeped in silence. I looked around the room and back to Clara, who was leaning on her desk, looking bored. The two men had disappeared back to the entrance of the warehouse. "The next job is in Barcelona-

Ryan

It was quick. So quick that I saw the flash from the barrel of the gun before I could even make sense of what was happening. Time froze as a piercing sound sent shock waves through my body that made me flinch. My ears ached with sharp pain, and I held my hands up to muffle the ringing that drilled my ear drums. Instinct caused me to duck my head, but my heart thumped against the walls of my chest as I looked around at Isabella. She was doing the same. Blood spilled on the floor as Clara stood over The Wolf's body. Her form was still firm, with an upright posture. I shuffled over to Isabella, who had regained her composure. She was about to fish a syringe out of her bag to stab it in Clara's neck when the two men came rushing to the small office. And with four more shots, their bodies tumbled limply to the ground, with blood pouring out of their heads and chests. Clara turned around and pointed the gun at us.

"These men were such arrogant pricks. Get up."

We slowly did as we were told. She instructed us to walk towards the back of the warehouse. There were two chairs in an empty room.

"Sit." She motioned to Isabella. "Put these on her." She threw some zip ties at me and instructed me to secure Isabella's hands and feet as she sat down. Isabella was passive. I couldn't tell if she was in shock or being strategic. I was certainly in shock but tried to keep it together. Clara instructed me to sit down and secured my hands and feet. When she was done, she dialled a number on her phone and spoke.

"It's done."

Isabella

It was too late to stick to the plan when I realised what had happened. Ryan had warned me to stay focused and in control. We had gone through the plan a few times, and I ensured the syringe was full of a lethal concoction to take The Wolf down. Not one to draw too much attention to myself in my killings, I decided that when the opportunity presented itself, I would make his death swift and straightforward. Then Clara would've followed him to the same grave. We hadn't known Clara had her own agenda, and she did the job much quicker and louder. One minute, The Wolf was rambling about Ryan and Andrew, and then his body was dead on the floor. I had to hand it to her, though; Clara was one crazy bitch. But now, Ryan and I were sitting on the most uncomfortable chairs ever while she rummaged around in my bag, pulling out the syringe and my phone.

"Pathetic." She tutted. "I sensed you would be up to something. And from my research sticking your victims with syringes is your speciality. Pity, guns beat syringes. Every time." We stayed silent.

"Where did you learn to shoot like that?" I eventually spoke, and Ryan shot me a look. She, on the other hand, ignored me. Ten minutes later, we heard footsteps approaching the room until a man walked in and kissed her. A frisson crept up my back when I instantly recognised him. He was the man I saw at the theatre Frank, Mik, Nathan, and I went to on New Year's Eve. I was right all along to feel on edge. The Wolf had eyes everywhere, but now I know that man was a double agent to execute Clara's agenda.

They quickly returned to Clara's office, and their voice slowly faded into a muffle. When they were out of sight, I tried to shuffle my way out of the zip ties, which was a stupid idea. I knew that it wouldn't help. However, I hated the feeling and realisation that I was momentarily helpless.

"Isabella, stop. You need to save your energy and keep your cool."

"I would've been calmer if you didn't tie these on so fucking tight!" I spat.

"There's a cutter in my pocket. Shuffle your chair to me and fish it out quickly." Time slowed for a second as Ryan said those words. I didn't want to admit that for a second; I thought my fate was doomed. My life had flashed before me with anticipation that crazy Clara would come back and pop us both in the head without hesitation. So, I pulled all my stretch to shuffle my chair close enough to him and tried to fish out the cutter as quickly as possible. The tool was small. Nonetheless, I was grateful that Ryan came prepared. Somehow, I managed to use the cutter to free myself from him.

"So you just walk around with zip tie cutters in your pocket?"

"For now, yes. I've worked for these people for years, Izzy. I know how they work. Trust me." He didn't need to say that. Since we returned from the Lake District, I knew I trusted him wholeheartedly.

"Now what?" My head was still foggy, but we had to find a way to escape this place.

"We find a way out and never look back."

We moved slow and low as though we were fugitives trying to escape in a cheesy crime thriller film. My heart was beating fast, but my will to live was strong, and my will to have us both survive this mess was stronger. As we walked towards an exit, I thought about how nice it would be to leave this city and go somewhere hot. I needed to do nothing but bathe on a beach and drink my body weight in champagne. Ryan grabbed my hand and lured me towards the closest exit; however, to get out of this place, we had to walk past Clara's office, where I heard her talking to the man from earlier. We halted and waited momentarily, contemplating how to slip out unnoticed.

"This is a mess babe!" He shouted, but she stood firm and held her composure. "You need to control your fucking impulses." He sighed and squeezed his eyebrows.

"I'll handle it." She stated without hesitation.

"The amount of shit that's going to land on us now!"

"I said I'll handle it!"

"No, WE will handle it. And we better clean up this mess fast or have your things ready to leave."

"I'm not going anywhere James. Stop talking to me in that tone or I'll handle you too." She walked to the and poured herself a drink whilst James exhaled a heavy sigh. He walked to her after a beat and wrapped her in his arms.

"I'm sorry. It's the stress." He kissed her neck and squeezed her tight. These people were of a different calibre to Ryan and me. They embraced their passion right next to The Wolf and his men's dead bodies without care for urgency. They continued to stand in an embrace, oblivious to our existence. For all I knew, they would come to 'handle' us once and for all. I squeezed Ryan's hand and took my chance to leap on Clara, grabbing her head from behind her head and tossing her body to the wall. Her body fell to the ground with a thud, but I didn't stop. This was my moment for revenge and freedom. At the same time, Ryan caught James by surprise and punched him multiple times before he fell to the ground. Just as he was about to stand, I saw the gun holstered in his lower back, so I quickly grabbed it.

"Stay right there." I pointed the gun at his head. "You too." Then, at Clara.

"That's not very clever Isabella." She spat.

"Oh you know how clever I can be Clara." I smirked at Ryan.

"We don't want any more trouble. We'll disappear and you'll never hear from us again." He finally spoke.

There was a long silence as they both sat in careful contemplation. I knew they would try to manipulate us. "Let's cut our losses here Clara. Go." James nodded. We were so close to the finish line. The exit was just out of through the office door, and I anticipated the relief of the fresh air, but then there was a loud noise. A gunshot. Clara had pulled the pistol from under her blazer and took a shot at me but missed. In retaliation, I pointed my gun to her face.

"You shot me in the leg first, I should just end your life right now." She stood frozen, and her forehead glistened with sweat.

"Enough." Ryan spoke. Still, I was consumed by the thirst for revenge. "Isabella. We don't need to do this anymore." And with his steady voice, Ryan pulled me out of the fog. He was right. Within an hour, we'd be out of this city forever, and they would never find us. I didn't need to kill her. She had killed herself by agreeing to work for The Wolf and then killing him. His loyal servants would be sure to avenge his death. I figured the scar on my leg would fade over a short time. I had a better outcome. I pointed the gun at her as we walked to the exit. As we approached the end of the interior, I heard Clara speak. Her voice was shaky and on the verge of breaking.

"I can't believe you let them go, we were supposed to run this shit together."

"Babe stop. It had to be done."

"NO!" She snapped, and the echo of her voice followed with a loud thud. A gunshot followed by the sound of her heels clicking on the floor. She was approaching fast, chasing us as we ran to freedom. We finally made it outside, where a black car with heavy-tinted windows waited. The back door opened as the driver's window rolled down.

"Hurry." Mik shouted as he started the engine. Clara was still approaching us, but we were already driving off in the car by the time she made it outside. She stood, determined yet defeated, lowered her hands and sighed. I took the opportunity to lower the window halfway and stuck out my middle finger to her.

Mik floored the gas, and her silhouette disappeared into the darkness within seconds.

Ryan

Of all the things I've been through. Of all the fights and near-death experiences I've had in my adult life, going through that with Isabella was worse. Not because I feared for my life but because I didn't want to lose her. Yes, she was tough and knew how to look after herself; however, Clara and The Wolf were a different breed of criminals. They looked glamorous, well-spoken and exuded silent confidence, and deep down, they were both rotten to the core. They possessed no heart or emotions of philosophy. There was no bargaining with them, and if you got too close, you'd soon find out just how cold they could be and how quickly they would kill. The Wolf thrived off having power, whilst Clara thrived off power. She leaned more on being motivated by money. Together, they alchemised into a perfect poison. The entire situation was a blur, but I do know that when I saw Isabella tied to that chair, frozen in shock, I knew that she needed to stay alive. I needed her alive. My life would be nothing without her. If I ever lost her, especially at the hands of someone else, I would never let it go. I would either go through the motions as an empty shell or spend the rest of my life recklessly avenging her death.

"We're nearly there." Mik's words pulled me from my thoughts, and I nodded.

"Where's there?" Isabella furrowed her eyebrows.

"We can't go back your apartment or my B&B, Clara would've sent her men there. Especially since we witnessed her slaying The Wolf. My bet is she's working hard to clean up and take over the organisation as we speak."

"I gathered that but where are we going?" She pressed.

"To a safehouse in Surrey." Her mouth dropped open.

"Surrey! We are a long way from Surrey, Ryan; what the

Mik floored the car before she finished her protest. The speed jolted us backwards and sideways in our seats. He looked at us in the rear-view mirror and smirked.

"This is not my first job Isabella. I'll get you there quickly. Trust me." And went silent again.

"Can I have a smoke?" She asked him, but her eyes shifted to a strange look that almost looked like desperation. Mike lit a cigarette and passed it to her. She rolled down the window and took a long draw.

Seeing her like this was surreal. I knew that she and Frank smoked weed and took illicit drugs. Hell, I've even indulged in a light session myself once or twice, but I had never seen her reach for a cigarette.

And as though she could read my mind, she said, "I only smoke these when I'm scared."

My heart dropped. Isabella had never been scared. Even in the face of trouble, she had always held herself up; her rage was unmatched, and her determination to survive was impossible to measure, but fear was never something she had shown or admitted. So I wrapped my arm around her and rested her head on my shoulder.

"You have nothing to be afraid of baby." I kissed her forehead. "I had planned this with Frank and Mik from when we were at the Lake District. They knew going to The Wolf would be a challenge and we agreed that no matter what happened, that you would escape and go far away from here. I swear to you Isabella. I know I messed up by leaving but I'm here with you now. I love you and won't ever let anything happen to you. Everything is set in place. Frank packed up your clothes, your assets and anything that was important to you are in the safehouse. Please, just trust us. Trust me." I held her tighter.

"It better be a nice house with a bath unlike that shack of a B&B you stayed in. I really need a bath." Both Mik and I burst out laughing. Just like that, my girl was back.

The rest of the journey was silent partly because we were tired and were processing the day's events. I, for one, needed a shower, some food and a bed. But if Isabella wanted to leave the country tonight, I told myself I would go with her. I was ready for that. Thirty minutes later, we arrived at the safe house in Surrey. I had arranged everything with Frank and Mik, from the pickup to the safehouse. I knew that regardless of the situation, Isabella would want to be comfortable and surrounded by luxury. The house was modest, but the giant windows created a luxurious atmosphere. The kitchen and bathroom were modern and new.

There was nothing to really complain about since I had planned for us to be there no longer than one week. Frank reassured me that all of Isabella's things would be brought there, and I was grateful for his and Mik's assistance. Mik had set up security cameras around the property in case trouble managed to cling onto our tail. We would inevitably be on our toes for the following days, and being stuck inside would probably take its toll, but we needed this time to lay low, regroup and make plans for our next move. Isabella had made it clear that she wanted to leave the country; the location was yet to be decided. All of my assets were remote in offshore accounts and safety deposits; just like Isabella, I was accustomed to having contingency plans. The most challenging thing about living this life was staying detached from places and faces. Faces such as Juliana and my old friends. The version of me they knew no longer existed. I was an outcast of society, and as much as I wanted a final catchup and goodbye, deep down, I knew that bluntly severing the connection was in the best interest of all parties.

Chapter Eleven

Isabella

The house was modest but nice. As much as I wanted to make a fuss, as I was out of my element of control, I had nothing to complain about. My things were neatly stored in boxes labelled with my name and contents. I didn't have many clothes or sentimental belongings, so the boxes were few, but they were items I had accumulated over time and couldn't stand to part ways with. I walked around the house and quickly familiarised myself with each room before peeling off my clothes and heading through the bedroom to the ensuite shower. Walking by the bed, I saw some pyjamas folded flat on there. Both bottom and top were matching colours, siren green cosy velour material inside and out. Next to them was a note.

I'm not there to snuggle with you, but these are the next best thing…Oh, and Ryan too. Frank x

I smiled. The day's stress had completely stolen my focus, but after seeing this note, I was reminded how much I missed my best friend. I was grateful for Ryan, but Frank was my rock. I quickly returned to the living room and went through the rest of the boxes. Sure enough, he had left me a new phone with his number saved in. My finger didn't hesitate to dial.

"I'm so glad you're alive." His voice was deep and soothing.

"I'm sorry to wake you. I just got to the house. Oh my god Frank, what a hell of a day." We both stayed silent for a beat.

"I'm just glad you're okay. We'll catch up, but for now, have a bath and relax in your new pyjamas." I giggled like a child, not because the conversation was funny but because I was so excited to hear his voice. "And enjoy the new pyjamas. I also left something for you in the kitchen cupboard." I walked to the kitchen and opened each cupboard until I saw a bottle of bourbon. It was the brand we always drank after a long day when we wanted a long night.

"Gosh you know me so well. Thank you for everything Frank. Thank you so much. I love you and I miss you. See you soon." I hung up before he could respond because we weren't the type to openly say shit like this to each other. We showed love through our actions, though, in that moment, I was at my most vulnerable and showing emotion was fitting.

I brought my attention back to the room when Ryan emerged with only a towel wrapped around his waist. His hair was still wet, exaggerating the brightness of his eyes. "I heard you on the phone, so I jumped in the shower first."

"I can see that." I walked towards him, traced my fingers down his chiselled torso, and continued to the bathroom, where I indulged in the best damn bath and shower of my life.

The following morning, I awoke with a sense of peace as though the day before didn't happen. Ryan and I went through the motions of drinking coffee and eating breakfast, which he cooked. A full English was something we both needed. We sat at the coffee table in the living room and admired the garden view through the giant windows. The squirrels hopped on the grass and leapt from trees as the birds tweeted, and the wind blew through the leaves.

"This isn't a bad place. But then again I've been living in a shack and rubbish B&B in the past months."

"I like it here, there's a nice silence. The city is so noisy."

"Maybe we'll find some place like this wherever we go."

Days passed, and we remained on edge. My nerves were taut, and each sound magnified in my ears. The safe house provided a semblance of security, but the knowledge that Clara and her people were still lurking in the shadows gnawed at us. We kept a watchful eye on the surveillance monitors that came installed with the house, scanning for any sign of intrusion. Ryan tried to pacify my anxiety, but everything he did made it worse. Just sitting and talking about it amplified the sense of doom. I yearned for the days when I could strap up my laces and run in the park, whether it was sunny or raining. Running was my outlet to get a clear head when my mind was cloudy. And when times were hard, I would suppress and numb the pain with drugs and alcohol. Right now, I didn't want any of those. I just needed space to breathe and be free. Frank and

Mik had come by every morning over the past few days to check in on me, and I appreciated the company. When the conversations dried up and the sunset glared through the woods, Ryan and I made love like never before. Every touch, kiss and moan was deeper than we had experienced, and each day we grew closer. At first, I thought that if this broke us, we would at least remain allies. However, we were now in the thick of it, and my heart had opened to swallow him whole.

"I love you." I would affirm and recite multiple times throughout the day, and he'd smile. "I love you too."

My usual night-time routine was interrupted as Ryan burst through the bedroom door. I had just gotten out of the shower and poured myself into shorts and an oversized t-shirt, ready to slump in our bed.

"There's someone in the garden." My heart froze for a moment as I knew who it would be. Clara was cunning, resourceful, and determined. Looking at the photos and documents from Detective Johnson's house, I knew that The Wolf and his people had always been one step ahead, and Clara was no exception. It didn't surprise me that she would send someone to infiltrate the safe house in the dead of night. My mind rounded back to reality as Ryan stood firm, glaring at me with apprehension. His presence felt safe, but his stern expression was a chilling reminder that we should never let our guard down; as long as we were in England, no place was truly safe. Out of instinct, though, I rushed into his arms, and our hearts raced as we heard a living room window break and within seconds, I heard the man step inside.

Ryan and I rushed to the kitchen. Fear ignited a fierce resolve within us. This was it. The intruder was merely a few steps away, and no doubt I knew he had a gun, but I didn't care. Our legs moved quickly, hearts catapulting as our breaths quickened for oxygen. My body was sweaty, knowing that we could die here, but I didn't care. We were fighting, and I would kill to protect this man. I rushed to the nearest drawer for a knife in the kitchen as Ryan launched himself at the intruder. He fought back, with his body moving with desperate agility. They both struggled and wrestled with each other for survival. My heart almost collapsed when the intruder towered over Ryan. His huge frame weighted him as he laid punches into him, and without time to think or hesitate, I ran and launched a sharp knife into his back. I had never done something like this, except for killing my stepdad with a baseball bat to defend my mother. At that moment, I felt the knife tear deep into the man's flesh, and the noise made me cringe. He shoved me to the floor before he quickly realised what had happened. And just then, Ryan got up and kicked him in the face so hard that the man's neck bent backwards, pulling the rest of his body with him. The room fell silent as he lay motionless on the floor.

With protective instinct, Ryan rushed to my side and traced his hand across my forehead, where a smidge of blood slowly trickled down. "Are you okay?" I nodded, too shocked to utter a word. He walked over to the body and stabbed the man again in the chest to ensure he was dead. "I'm sorry to do this in front of you. I know you prefer a cleaner kill, but we must be thorough." I stared at him, wide-eyed.

The adrenaline had washed over me, and I was manic. Shockwaves of emotions coursed through me. One minute, I was calm, and the next, I was shaky. I held onto the tumbler of bourbon in my hands like it was a lifeline. Ryan wrapped a blanket around my shoulders as he went for a quick surveillance patrol around the house. When he came back, he confirmed the coast was clear. "And what do we do with him?"

"I've called Frank and Mik to help me take the trash out." I fell silent. "Hey." He came and knelt before me like I was a troubled child. And I guess I was inside. "I know you're in shock, and the past few days have been a lot. I need you to keep it together. I will do everything in my power to protect you, Isabella, but I need you to keep your chin up."

I nodded. He was right. The past few months had been a whirlwind of events that led us to this moment. We were nearly at the finish line, and I'd be damned if I let that bitch Clara hurt me again.

I stirred and opened my eyes to find myself tucked under the duvet in our bed. The morning sun peeked through the crack of the curtain. The space next to me was empty, and my head ached. In a slight panic, I climbed out of bed and walked to the kitchen to find Ryan, Mik and Frank standing there. I rushed into my best friend's arms and buried my face in his chest. He held me tight and silently caressed my hair. I was sure Mik and Ryan were staring, but I didn't care. Frank was my best friend, and I needed his comfort to refuel my strength. A few seconds later, the cracks in my façade split open. I broke down and burst into tears right there in the arms of my best friend, his boyfriend and in front of the man I loved. I didn't care because I needed a release. All the years of keeping it together and hardening my heart as a mask for survival came apart in front of the three most important men in my life. I was ugly, crying, too. Snot dripped out of my nose as my eyes swelled with tears. Then, something remarkable happened; Frank held me tighter whilst Mik and Ryan rushed around the kitchen; one collected tissue and the other made a pot of tea. Frank carried me to the sofa to soothe and wipe my tears. They all gathered around me like three pillars, and they became my strength.

"I can't do this anymore. I don't want to be here. I'm scared." I said or rather mumbled through the lumps in my throat. They listened intently, rubbed my back and encouraged me to drink hot tea. A few minutes later, I had calmed down, but the room stayed silent, which was when I realised it had been cleaned and the body had disappeared. The window was also fixed, and the house looked spotless, as though nothing had happened. For the first time, I felt the ease of relinquishing control. I trusted that these men were in my life through thick and thin.

"Izzy we know you don't want to be here anymore. You've told us a million times. Everything is taken care of and going according to plan, minus the minor interruption." Frank smirked.

"Yes, baby we're leaving tonight."

"Tonight?" I managed a whisper.

"Yeah, tonight. I know you played with the idea of moving to France but that's way too close. We're going to the Bahamas."

A pang of sadness gripped my heart. I knew that my best friend would have to remain behind. The dangerous web we had become entangled in had irreversibly altered our lives. And as much as I wanted to be near Frank every day, I knew it was time to leave.

The hours went by quickly. There wasn't much to do except discuss departure plans with Frank and Mik. New passports and necessary documents have been created for Ryan and me. The guys had ensured everything was seamless, from the names used to the place we'd be living in, until we decided to move on. The thought of having the opportunity to travel the world without care excited me. But in the immediate future, I wanted to settle and take a reprieve.

"Are you ready?" Mik had floored the car to the airport in the early evening hours. A private jet was waiting, and all the necessary arrangements had been put in place. Standing at the gate, I took a moment to take in Frank's frame. He was bigger than before, and his face had filled out, but it suited him. I took comfort in knowing that he was truly happy with Mik and that they would come to visit when we had settled.

"I'm going to miss you. Thank you for everything." We made our final embrace before I tearfully retracted and made my way through the gate, holding Ryan's hand.

"Keep my woman happy Ryan. I'll be checking in." Frank smiled.

On the plane, Ryan never let go of my hand. He said he would always protect and comfort me, and since he knew I was nervous, he kept a close eye on me. We had to leave it all behind and start anew. The Bahamas beckoned, promising a fresh start and a chance to rebuild our shattered lives.

Two Weeks Later

Our new home was lovely. We never had to worry about money since we both had squirrelled a lot of it in offshore accounts, so we took the time to slow down and decompress. We made love all over the villa and sunbathed most of the day. I got back into my meditation and workout routine quickly, which Ryan decided to join in on most days. My mind, battered spirit, and body had begun to heal, and I was starting to feel like myself again. As we settled into our new home in the Bahamas, the weight of our journey began to lift. We marvelled at the pristine beaches, the turquoise waters lapping at the shore. Our love, once fraught with danger, had found solace in this idyllic paradise.

One late afternoon, As I stood on the veranda enjoying the fresh sea air, my heart skipped a beat. Approaching the villa were familiar faces. I froze in shock and disbelief. It was Frank and Mik. This couldn't be real, I thought. I had missed them like crazy, and I yearned for the time I'd be able to see them again just as much as I mourned the happy days in our past when we stayed up late and talked shit until we passed out. As they approached closer and their shape became prominent, I knew this wasn't a dream. So I ran to them and jumped into Frank's arms.

"Oh my god!" I couldn't contain my excitement. Ryan emerged from inside the villa to see what was happening. He calmly walked up to them and shook their hands.

"Welcome to your new home."

"You're staying?" I squeaked. "And you knew about this?" I turned to Ryan.

"We all knew about this Izzy. Of course, I would never dream of living life without you. London is overrated and Mik fancied an early retirement. We just needed things to cool down first and tie up some loose ends." I stood in shock. Tears started falling down my cheeks, and I was crying again. But this time, it was with happiness.

My sadness transformed into an overwhelming sense of gratitude and love at that moment. Together, we embraced the weight of our shared journey, lifting it from our shoulders. The future was uncertain, but we knew that with each other, we could face whatever challenges lay ahead. Although the only ones I could think of were where we would travel to next. As I was about to usher them inside, I heard a noise from Frank's bag. He opened the flap to reveal a carrier, and inside, looking fluffy and gorgeous, was Jules, our rescue kitten who had turned into a giant fluffball.

And so, as the sun dipped below the horizon, casting a golden glow, Ryan, Frank, Mik, and I toasted to new beginnings, cherishing the freedom we had fought so hard to secure. In the warm embrace of the Bahamas, we vowed to live our lives to the fullest, forever grateful for the love and loyalty that had us through the darkest times. I also vowed to open my heart and love Ryan fully. It had been a rough ride, but we made it to our version of heaven, and that's all that mattered.

Book Four

END

Books by J.P. Mooney

A Virgo's Point of You
Prose for those seeing the world for what it truly is
**The Ups and Downs of Winning Series, Book
Three**

F*CK You, I'm Tired
Prose for navigating the politics of life
**The Ups and Downs of Winning Series, Book
Two**

F*CK You, I'm Fabulous
Prose for the bold
**The Ups and Downs of Winning Series, Book
One**

Broken Petals:
Inside the cracks of lust infused desires
Mated Fortune Series, Book three

Beautiful Jaded Butterflies:
Sometimes love is nothing but a twisted game of
chess
Mated Fortune Series, Book Two

Isabella:
Crime has never looked this fabulous **Mated
Fortune Series, Book One**

Poetry For The Awakened:

Ley Lines
Poetry for the certified warrior

tiny reads:
A poetry collection for on the go spirits

Prana: Poems of the Moment

Virgo's Carousel:
Are you brave enough for the ride?

Mercury Retrograde Poems: Climbing off the Ferris Wheel

Available on Amazon